Neil Smith, Maureen Bilerman & Jaspreet Singh

COMING ATTRACTIONS
04

We acknowledge the support of the Canada Council for the Arts, the Ontario Arts Council, the Government of Ontario through the Ontario Media Development Corporation's Book Publishing Tax Credit program and the Government of Canada through the Book Publishing Industry Development Program for our publishing activities.

"The Butterfly Box" by Neil Smith first appeared in *The Antigonish Review*; "Isolettes" by Neil Smith was originally published in *The Malahat Review* and is forthcoming in the *Journey Prize Anthology*; "Green Fluorescent Protein" by Neil Smith was first published in Event and in the *Journey Prize Anthology*; "Getaway" by Maureen Bilerman won first prize in the New Brunswick Literary Competition; "Spellbound," "A Little Bit of Bar-rough" and "You Must Be" by Jaspreet Singh first appeared in *Fiddlehead*.

ISBN 0 7780 1256 5 (hardcover)
ISBN 0 7780 1257 3 (softcover)

Cover art by David Helwig
Book design by Michael Macklem

Printed in Canada

PUBLISHED IN CANADA BY OBERON PRESS

Contents

INTRODUCTION

Throw the TV and telephone in the wading pool, tape tinfoil on your trailer windows, tear open these pages and behold; feast your tired eyes on these shining jewels, these stylish story tellers from very different planets.

Neil Smith, nominated for a National Magazine Award and for the Journey Prize, has created a dazzling style, jumpy and kinetic with amazing diction that is as unexpected as it is electric. Writing piercing stories that break the mould to live and die by their skill with language, he is a young master of the form.

Maureen Bilerman explores with humour and melancholy the knotty forces of nature and eros, using striking images and surprising metaphors to convey her characters' travails and slippery lack of satisfaction on the boondock back-roads. The urban and rural coexist uneasily in her finely shaded tales of whitewater canoeing and salmon fishing and puzzled couples teasing out the mysteries of nature, the head and heart.

Jaspreet Singh writes in a unique endearing voice about romance and big science, and the affairs and laws that dominate both odd worlds. His characters travel the globe—Kashmir, India, Wisconsin, Montreal, Banff—pilgrims searching for some solution just out of reach, exploring and experimenting with their lives and work, erudite exiles drawn with sensuous empathy.

This is a vintage year for Coming Attractions: three exciting new writers unfolding nine stories of unease and family and flawed romance and whimsy and wit, tearing their pleasures with rough strife through the iron gates, and taking us along for the ride.

MARK ANTHONY JARMAN

Contributions for Coming Attractions 05, *published or unpublished, should be sent to Oberon Press, 205–145 Spruce Street, Ottawa, Ontario* KIR 6PI *before 31 March, 2005. All manuscripts should enclose a stamped self-addressed envelope.*

NEIL SMITH

The Butterfly Box

I remember posing for my father. The first time, I was five years old.

That afternoon, my mother had whirled our dachshund's food bowl across the kitchen, clipping my father on the chin. Then she crammed her suitcases into her Rambler and squealed off down the street. When Fred slunk out of his studio, I was making thumb imprints in the gobs of Alpo on the linoleum. He towelled off my hands and plunked me down on the chesterfield.

He didn't lie to me. He didn't say, "She'll be back." He hardly spoke a word. He simply went to get his sketchpad so he could capture my look of bewilderment.

Skip ahead sixteen years and here I am again, posing. It's the opening night of Fred's retrospective. But it's my retrospective too. When I pose I reminisce.

I'm posing downtown in the display window at the Nurani Art Gallery. It was the Curator's idea to place my old bed, our tiffany floor lamp and our chipped wooden armoire in the window just as they're arranged in one of Fred's paintings.

The guy in the window with the corkscrew hair and coffee-bean eyes is me. I'm sitting cross-legged on the bed with a shallow, glass-lid case in my lap. Pinned inside the case is Polyommatus icarus. A Common Blue. One of the dozens of butterflies I collected as a kid.

My eyes drift toward a sign hanging in the display window. The sign faces outward so its words appear to people passing in the street. It says: FRED ROBERTSON, 1991, THE BUTTERFLY BOX.

To me it reads like an epitaph.

I live in the town of Hammond, which isn't far from the

city—just a hop, skip and a dump, as Fred was fond of saying. Mine is that two-storey brick home with the thicket of peeling birch trees out front and a porch so sunken it seems to smile at you from the street.

The day Fred sketched out *The Butterfly Box*, I was sixteen, scrawny as a Giacometti sculpture. My father sat me down on my bed. He straightened my shoulders and raked the bangs from my forehead.

He sat across from me in his tie and blazer and polished oxblood shoes. His sketching clothes. You'd have thought he was running a bank instead of doodling for a living.

As I watched his pencil figure-skate across the sketchpad, I began daydreaming of a trek we'd taken to the Painted Desert in Arizona the summer before.

"Hey, Jack," Fred whispered. "Stop your fidgeting." I was stock-still. It was our running joke: he knew his fingers would cramp up before I'd lose a pose.

"Want to know how I'd draw?" I ventriloquized.

"Enlighten me." His thumb smudged graphite across the page.

"Take a photograph of an image. Trace a grid over top, with boxes one inch by one inch. In your sketchpad, draw another grid with boxes two inches by two inches. Using the grid lines as your guide, clone your image—the same but bigger."

Fred ping-ponged his eyes between me and his sketchpad. "Wouldn't you be boxing yourself in?"

Well, that was the idea.

A few days later, I tried my technique. I pulled out a *National Geographic* with an article on the Monarch's winter journey to Mexico. I tore out a full-page picture and traced my grid over top. In a sketchbook, I duplicated *Danaus plexippus*, erased the grid lines, and then coloured in the butterfly wings with orange and black magic markers.

"What do you think?"

"Not bad at all," Fred said.

"Don't lie to me, man. It's as lifelike as a bug squashed against a windshield."

"There's life here."

Fred placed my sketch against the window in his studio and the sunlight lit it up like stained glass. Then he bent the sides of the sketch back and forth till the Monarch fluttered its wings and took flight.

"Can you see it now?"

"Ollie-Ollie-oxen-free."

I look up and see the Curator's man-in-the-moon face poking through the curtain that hems in the back of the window display.

"Excuse me?"

The Curator's wire Ben Franklin glasses hop down his nose. "I mean you can come out now."

I met the Curator at Fred's first show at the Nurani. I was twelve and had called him the Mortician because we'd just attended my great-aunt's funeral the week before. Honest mistake, Fred admitted. They both deal in the remains of the dead.

The Curator steps into the display window and lowers his rump onto the bed. He sighs wistfully.

"Jack, your father's work is a wonderful empirical means of suspending the flow of time."

This is how the art world sweet-talks.

"Fred's with us," says the Curator. His breath has the vernissage smell of Camembert cheese and green grapes. "He's thankful so many people are here admiring his work."

Many of the guests are probably ticked off they didn't buy sooner before the value shot up.

The Curator tugs a handkerchief from his blazer pocket and cleans his glasses as people pass in the street. Three Girl Scouts plaster themselves against the window like gecko lizards.

The Curator pats my hand and stands up to go. "Maybe

you'd prefer visiting the exhibition after everyone leaves."

I nod.

The only thing better than an art exhibit without the people is an art exhibit without the art.

In the summertime, Fred had a break from the modern art classes he taught at Underwood College. He'd spend his days hidden away in his studio, a hump-like addition on the back of the house that we called Quasimodo.

One summer day, I bicycled home after my shift at Critters, the local pet shop, and joined Fred in the studio.

"Hey, you're getting musty, man," I said. "You need an airing."

He glanced up, foggy-eyed, from a canvas. Beside him, his tubes of paint were cued up by hue.

"How about a walk?" I asked. Alice B, our arthritic dachshund, click-clacked toward me across the hardwood floor.

"Maybe later."

"Listen, you haven't been outside in three days. You haven't spoken to a soul but me in two weeks."

"A lecture on socializing from a guy whose best friend is a Red Admiral butterfly."

Ignoring this, I scooped up Alice B in my arms. "Look what our daddy has painted today," I said in a needling baby voice. I pointed the dog's snout toward the canvas. "Look at that pretty lady. Such a pretty lady for daddy."

Fred sighed and laid his brush down.

We ended up walking to Necropolis, the name he'd given to the cemetery in town. We sat down on the graves, Fred beside Cordelia Feltwell's tombstone (REMEMBER ME IS ALL I ASK) and me beside George Kingston Sr.'s (TO LOVE IS TO BURY). Willow trees swayed in the breeze like giant hula dancers.

"Feeling loquacious, Jack?" Fred wanted me to talk.

"Guess how Cordelia died," I said after a moment. "One

evening the old lush sets up the blender on the side of the tub. She wants to mix up daiquiris while soaking in her bubble bath. After her third drink, she knocks the blender into the water, creates a new cocktail—a Cordelia cordial."

Fred rolled his eyes and mouthed a Camel from his cigarette pack.

"Then there's George Kingston." I nodded toward the tombstone with its crumbling parade of angels. "He's a Mormon minister preaching polygamy. That is, till his two wives fall for each other, ditch him, and make a killing co-inventing the plastic nibs on the end of shoelaces. The envy does him in."

Fred scratched his beard and stared at me. "You know, Jack, they can do wonders today with electroshock."

"So what's your story?" I said. "How you gonna kick off?"

Fred dragged on his Camel and eyed Alice B, who was yapping at a caterpillar crawling up Cordelia's tombstone.

"This is how I want to go," he said. "I'm a butterfly sailing from flower to flower. Blissfully happy 'cause from larva to imago I've done exactly as I've pleased. Suddenly a net snaps down, whips me into the killing jar. In three seconds flat, an odourless gas has lulled me to sleep."

I threw a stick across the graveyard and Alice B hobbled after it. Then I placed my finger in the caterpillar's path. It stepped aboard. From the blond punk-rock spikes on its back, I could tell it would metamorphose into *Colias croceus*. A Clouded Yellow.

"You know, Fred, the ancient Greeks believed that after death the soul flew from the body as a butterfly."

Fred stuck his face up close to my outstretched hand. He dragged on his cigarette and puffed a whiff of smoke at the caterpillar. It rolled up like a sleeping bag.

How many stories like this make up a retrospective?

Sitting mannequin-stiff on my bed, I watch the guests

drift out of the art gallery. Some stop and point or greet me with little Queen Elizabeth waves.

From behind the curtain comes the Curator's voice. "Is our jack-in-the-box ready to take a look around?"

Goosepimply ominous—that's how one reviewer described Fred's work. My father liked that. He wanted his paintings to be snapshots of the windless calm before an earthquake hits.

As I walk into the exhibit hall, that's the calm I feel. The hall is long and narrow with wooden floor slats that seem to converge at its far end. Fred's canvases are hung on the walls in clusters.

In *Barbershop*, a man draped in a sheet sits waiting for a trim. Next to him, a tangle of scissors soak in a jar. In *Push Me Higher*, a barefoot woman with a lopsided smile sits on a playground swing.

What I like is looking at Fred's paintings up close. So close, say, that the hand gripping that playground swing bursts into a dapple of yellows and oranges and licks of navy.

The woman on the swing is Judy. She was my boss at Critters and, for a few months, Fred's girlfriend and muse. In fact, all my father's muses grace the paintings hung around the hall. There's Samantha with her Dada tattoos, including a furry teacup in her armpit. On the far wall is Teresa, a potter from Mexico who taught me to differentiate smells of clay. Next to her, we have Diane, a cookbook writer who put Fred and me on a vegan diet that left us lactose intolerant. None of these women remained in the picture very long. The day Diane dumped my father, she said that if her love life were a meal Fred would be melba toast—a flat, tasteless appetizer.

So with the muses always disappearing who stepped in to pose when it came time to paint? The arms cradling that jug of milk in *Elimination Diet*, the shoulder-blade under

15

that tattoo in *Indelible Ink*, those strained calves, the nape of that neck, even the hand grasping the playground swing. Scattered all over the room are pieces of me.

In the last canvas I come to, these pieces merge. There I am, sitting on my bed, my head cocked sideways. In my lap is the butterfly box. I tilt it up but the glass front of the box acts as a mirror so that what appears is not a Red Admiral or a Clouded Yellow or a Common Blue. What appears is the reflected face of the artist staring back. My father, transfixed by his own reflection.

Enough, I think. Enough.

I walk out of the hall and come face to face with a publicity poster for the exhibit. It's Fred's profile with his name printed across the bottom. Underneath his name is a date: 1948— . I stare at this date. A prickly blush creeps across my face as I realize how much I want that empty space filled.

An autumn afternoon a year and eleven months ago. Fred and I were lazing in the backyard on what I jokingly called our *chaises longues*. I was reading a book on ferret breeding. Fred was sulking through a funk. The reason? Maybe a quarrel with a muse, a stack of student papers to mark, a canvas gone awry.

"Robertson's blue period, I presume," I mumbled.

He turned away from me in his lawn chair. A handful of change spilled from the pocket of his smock and jingled onto the patio.

"I'll head inside and make supper," I said and put my book down. I planned to make tacos and cornbread, Fred's favourites. "You stay outside awhile. You need the fresh air."

"For Christ's sake," Fred snapped. "You're the opposite of a mamma's boy. You're a boy mamma. You sure I don't need a sweater in case it turns cold?"

I scowled at him and went inside. In the kitchen, I tore

apart a head of lettuce. I grated the cheddar cheese with such force I decapitated a wart on my thumb. Yet by the time the cornbread was baked, wouldn't you know I was whistling along to the oldies station.

The oven had heated the kitchen up and so I went to the back window and hoisted it open. Across the lawn I could see Fred. He was kneeling on the ground beside a grove of birch trees. He was looking straight at me through the window.

I waved and thought, beautiful composition—the shimmering grass, the still trees, Fred in his paint-speckled smock. Then I noticed his mouth. It was opening and closing soundlessly like the puffer fish in their tanks at the pet shop.

In two seconds, I was out the door but already he was face down in the grass.

Before heading home, I climb back into the display window to pick up the butterfly box. I sit down on the bed and consider slipping between the covers and spending the night.

The Common Blue looks up at me, its wings flaring like a blowtorch flame.

"Why not go see him tonight?" I imagine it saying. "You hardly ever drop by anymore."

In the corridor, I pass an empty stretcher and orderlies in running shoes. It's the same toothpaste-coloured corridor I've walked down countless times before. When I reach his room I stop, glance through the window, and drum my fingers against the glass.

I see the monitor with the zigzagging line, like a seismograph measuring aftershocks. I see the plastic tubing and respirator. I open the door, walk into this room. I step up close. Close enough to see the capillaries in his earlobe, the flick of an eyelid, the gentle rising of his chest.

17

When you die and are put into the ground, your fingernails continue to grow. And so do his. So I tug open the drawer of the bedside table and fish around for the clipper. Then I pick up his hand and feel its warmth. One by one, I clip his nails and heap the little crescent moons into a pile on his chest.

When I'm finished, I draw up a chair and sit. I ask him questions—"Any news from Cordelia Feltwell?"—and then make up his replies as the IV drips into a vein in his wrist.

Later a nurse taps a knuckle against the window. She points to her wristwatch: visiting hours are over.

I stand, stretch, and then bend over the bed to pull the blanket up. Fred's arm jumps and knocks my hand away. It's only a spasm.

"Stop your fidgeting," I say.

Isolettes

Blue tube, green tube, clear tube, fat tube. A Dr. Seuss rhyme. The tubes run from robotic Magi gathered around the incubator, snake through portholes in the clear plastic box, then burrow into the baby's pinkish grey skin. One tube up her left nostril. One tube down her throat. One tube into an arm no wider than a Popsicle stick. One tube tunnels into her chest. The skin of her chest seems so thin. The baby's mother can almost see the tiny organs beneath, the way shrimp is visible under the rice paper of a spring roll. The baby doesn't move. Doesn't cry. To the mother, the baby, with its blue-black eyes, is an extraterrestrial crash-landed on her planet. Hidden away and kept alive by G-men while they assess what threat this tiny alien might pose.

"What kind of mother will you be?" Jacob asked. He and An sat side by side on a braided rug watching a flickering candle on An's coffee table. An said, "I won't be a mommy who bores people with the trials and tribulations of teething." Jacob disagreed: "You'll be like those TV-com-mercial moms who fret over whether to buy two-ply or three-ply toilet paper." From the coffee-table, An picked up a blue ceramic cup, the kind used for espresso, and handed it to Jacob. "Real traditional," she said, "real Norman Rockwell." Jacob grinned and stood. He had long coltish legs. While he was in the bathroom, An dropped a jazz CD into her player and then went into her bedroom and lay on her bed. Before the first song ended, Jacob came out of the bathroom. "You were fast this time," An said. Jacob replied he'd been practising at home. He handed her the espresso cup and kissed her forehead. "I don't love you," he said. An replied, "I don't love you, too." After he'd let himself out of the apartment, An drew Jacob's semen into a syringe. She hiked up her peasant skirt and slid off her underwear. Then she lay on her bed, two pillows propped beneath her rear. It was the first time with the pillows: gravity, she reasoned, would help.

Neonatal Intensive Care Unit. Otherwise known as N.I.C.U. The doctors pronounce it NICK U, as if it were a university. "Our kid is studying at NICK U," Jacob jokes with a nurse, who stares at him blankly. An thinks of NICK U as a baby hatchery, one that smells like the stuff dentists use to clean teeth. The incubators, a dozen aquariums, are not in neat rows, but here and there the way progressive school teachers arrange desks. Ventilators hum, monitors flash, alarms sound, a baby makes a noise like a gobbling turkey. Meanwhile, neonatologists complete their rounds. Some spill a hot alphabet-soup of acronyms—ROP, BPD, C-PAP—in An's lap. Others say with a hand on her shoulder: "We realize how stressful this must be." To them all, An wants to yell: "Nick you!" Better yet: "Nick off and die!"

Four months into An's pregnancy, Jacob moved into a top-floor apartment in her building. He called the place the *pent-up* suite, because according to An, the former tenants, a sulky husband and wife, were passive-aggressives. To exorcise the couple's demons, Jacob wandered around his stacks of moving boxes spritzing a citrus deodorizer. "If marriage is an institution," he said, "married people should be institutionalized." An wondered if this was a veiled reminder: that she and Jacob were not a couple, that they weren't bookends propping up *Dr. Spock's Baby and Childcare*. Still, the move into her building was Jacob's idea. An concurred, though. Proximity without intimacy: it sounded good to her. She had no desire to actually live with Jacob or any other man. Men's bathroom habits, the Q-Tips caked with earwax they left on the sink, depressed her. "Maybe more marriages would last if couples didn't live together," she said to Jacob as he unpacked a food processor the size of a space probe. "Maybe couples should buy a semi-detached and each live on either side," she added. Jacob laughed his nose-honking laugh. "That's why you always strike out at love, An," he said. "You're so semi-detached."

Between the twenty-third and twenty-fourth week of An's pregnancy, the placenta began to separate from the uterine wall. Semi-detached, An thought, when the doctor told her. By this time, she was lying under a spotlight in the emergency ward of the Royal Victoria Hospital. Her contractions were a minute apart. A nurse, the one who'd injected her with antibiotics earlier, yelled out, "Cervix fully effaced!" The warm amniotic fluid trickled over An's thighs and the obstetrician soon announced, "She's crowning," as if An herself were Queen Victoria. Then came the huge irresistible urge to push. When the neonatologist lifted her newborn daughter, An saw the tiny baby bat the air with one arm as if to clear everyone away, the doctors, the nurses —even her exhausted, terrified mother.

Though An hadn't wanted a baby shower, Jacob gave her one anyway. The theme, fittingly, was showers. The weather co-operated by drizzling. First, they took in the stage musical *Les Parapluies de Cherbourg* co-starring An's mother, Lise, who played an umbrella-shop owner in Normandy who meddled in her daughter's affair with a kind-hearted mechanic. The daughter got pregnant by the mechanic but ended up marrying a diamond importer she didn't love but grew to respect. During the standing ovation, Jacob whispered, "Only the French can make a *comédie musicale* depressing." Backstage, Lise pulled An into her dressing-room and shut the door. Her stage makeup was as cracked as a Rembrandt. Lise sat at her vanity, pulled bobby pins from her soufflé of a wig, and talked to An's reflection about the play's theme. "Not only passion and true love, but more subtle kinds of love and devotion and attachment." She talked loudly as if she were still on stage. "You want me to marry a diamond importer?" An joked. Lise tossed her wig at An. "What I'm saying is I'm trying to understand." An thanked her mother for making an effort—an effort that deflated when An opened the dressing-room door. In the hall, Jacob was talking to the mechanic, his hand on the actor's thigh. "Watch out for that one," Lise yelled to the mechanic. "He'll ejaculate into anything."

"What's your baby's name, honey?" the big woman asks. She has crinkly permed hair and fleshy arms like hams. "Haven't thought of one yet," An mumbles. The woman sits down beside An in the lounge outside NICK U. The chair creaks under her weight. Sheila's her name. She delivered a 29-weeker. "We wanted to call our son Alek," she explains, "but he was born all pink and mewing and tiny like a newborn kangaroo, so we named him Joey." An has seen the sign taped to his incubator: HI EVERYONE, MY NAME'S JOEY. Many of the incubators are personalized with signs. You can even stick stuffed animals through an incubator's porthole the way you'd place a treasure chest at the bottom of a fish tank. An tells Sheila she's afraid to name her baby, that naming her might be a jinx. An is surprised at herself: for saying such a thing (she's not superstitious) and for revealing something to a stranger. It must be exhaustion, or too many peanut-butter cups from the vending machine. Sheila grabs An's hand and squeezes. "No, no, no," she insists. "Naming your baby will encourage her to live." Above Sheila's head is a poster of a baker frosting a cake with the letter B. The pattycake, pattycake man. "What about B?" An says. "Bea!" Sheila squeals and then adds: "Short for Beatrice. Like Beatrix Potter—nothing bad ever happens in Beatrix Potter!"

An's own name started as Anne Brouillette-Kappelhoff, the last name a coupling of her French-Canadian mother's and her German father's. When Anne was in high school, she often signed her papers Anne B-K to rein in her unwieldy name. By the time she hit university, she'd also sliced two letters off her first name. "A N," she'd spell. "Like the indefinite article." It got people's attention. Made them think her eccentric, and at 21, looking fourteen, that's what she wanted. While her friends dressed in black, she wore flowery Laura Ashley dresses, accented with green Doc Martens lace-up boots. In her creative writing class, she handed in "Gee Your Hair Smells Terrific," a story about a crazed Avon lady who drowned a suburban housewife in a bubble bath. A boy in the class, who wore a spiked dog collar and an alligator polo shirt, liked the story very much. It was different, he said, from the "ethereal lyrical namby-pamby schlock" that the other girls handed in. The other girls began to hate this boy, whose name was Jacob.

Jacob sings "Supercalifragilisticexpialidocious" to B because he says she's so precocious. He waves to her through the plastic. She is four days old and weighs 520 grams, about the weight of the two sweet potatoes An bought for supper last night. Every day B gains the weight of a penny. "She's got your wrinkly forehead," Jacob says to An, who sits in a moulded plastic chair next to the incubator, smoothing out the yellow robe all the parents wear and twiddling the plastic bracelet that reads MOTHER 87308. Across from them, Sheila sits with her robe open and her blouse lifted. Joey, who's now two months old, cuddles against her stomach, skin-to-skin contact that the nurses call kangaroo care. Sheila is humming "You Are the Sunshine of My Life" because Stevie Wonder was a preemie. An gets up and paces the room. She goes out the door of NICK U and into the elevator and down to the lobby and out the front door. A pregnant woman is waddling in. Little head, huge belly, like an upside-down question mark: ¿. A single sob jumps from An's throat, and the woman throws her a startled look. An goes over to the bike rack in the hospital's parking-lot and sits on a purple ten-speed with a banana seat. It's not hers but it looks like the bike she had as a kid. It's a spring day, sunny but chilly. She breathes slowly and deeply through her nose as in her yoga class. After a half hour, she feels almost serene. She goes back up to NICK U where FATHER 87308 has become a thespian. "To B or not to B," he drones to his daughter.

On stage was a stripper dressed in a fireman's yellow coat and rubber boots. The costume made dancing difficult, but he tried, shuffling back and forth to a rap song whose refrain went: "Don't blame me if your mental age is three." An's librarian friend Catou screwed up her face and said, "How could you have agreed to this?" She meant Part II of An's shower, which was held in a strip club called Wet. In the middle of the stage was a see-through shower stall where the fireman, now naked, was soaping his chest as water drizzled over him. Jacob had reserved a spot to one side of the stage. There, gathered around two tables pushed together, were eight of An's friends, a couple of translators and a few academics from the university where Jacob taught Russian lit. In the middle of the table was a stack of baby gifts: teething rings, pyjamas with the feet in, a duckie mobile. Jacob held his gift over his head: a clown doll the size of a ventriloquist's dummy with a bulbous nose and a wreath of rainbow hair. Mr. Pinkelton was his name. Jacob pressed the doll's belly, and Mr. Pinkelton emitted a phlegmy smoker's hack. Catou told An that she had met a real clown that week, a social worker who dressed as Bozo to read to children at the library. "He's single and he loves kids," Catou said. "I could set you up." An replied, "I'm six months pregnant, for Christ's sake." Up on stage, the stripper wagged his genitals like a clown twisting a dachshund out of party balloons.

When An agreed to Catou's blind dates in the past, she would often see something in the man's eyes. Not passion but more a yearning for passion. She, however, could never drum up the same enthusiasm. The whole scene always smacked of play-acting, like those histrionic *téléromans* her mother starred in. The dates made her want to laugh; she did laugh in a few men's faces. One called her a cold fish, which made her laugh harder. So she'd given up on relationships, although she'd never really given *in* to them. Jacob said she was like a two-cigarette-a-day smoker who'd kicked the habit.

One of these dates, a Korean immigrant still struggling with idiom, asked An, "What do you do for the living?" With a stranger, small talk often kicks off with your job. So that's where An begins when she eventually leans over the incubator to introduce herself to B. "My name's An and I'm a translator," she whispers. She admits to B that she'd always hoped to work at something creative. "Drawing, writing, acting—I have some talent," she says. "But sometimes no talent is better. It saves you from expending so much energy when the best you can hope for is above average." She explains that, in university, she majored first in English lit. But the professors were so fiercely intelligent their IQs left scratch marks on her ego, and so she switched over to translation. She now works freelance from home, mostly subtitling television documentaries. In her job, she shrinks people's words down to a pithy sentence that fits on the screen. "But B, who am I to put words in their mouths," she whispers, "when most of the time, I barely understand what *I'm* trying to say?" Across the room, Sheila spies An talking to B and gives a thumbs-up. Translation: Finally!

Sheila is not the type of woman An usually befriends. Not once in her life has Sheila uttered the word "paradigm." Sheila lives in a suburban bungalow. She shows photos of this bungalow to An before taping them to Joey's incubator, picture side against the plastic. "So he'll feel at home," she tells An. To her skinny marsupial baby, she promises, "Someday you'll have your father's beer belly and my fat ass." Like the neonatologists, she makes her rounds, visiting the other parents, asking questions. In the Pattycake Lounge (as An has dubbed it), she calls Jacob An's "hubby." And so An explains. Sheila's eyes grow even rounder behind her fishbowl glasses. A father who is sitting nearby and who calls the mother of his child "the wife" mutters, "That doesn't sound very natural." An is too weary to argue, but not Sheila. She gets up and throws open the door to NICK U, exposing the battery of machines keeping their children alive. "Show me one thing in there that's natural!"

Natural air is about 21 % oxygen. That's what Dr. Amelios, the neonatologist, is telling An and Jacob. B lies in her incubator, a tiny stocking cap wiggled onto her head to help conserve body heat. The clear tube down her throat is her air tube. B wrenches her head sideways as if to free herself. "This baby is state-of-the-art," Dr. Amelios says, and till he pats a hand against the ventilator contraption, An thinks he's referring to B. "It oscillates fast so it does little damage to the lungs," he says. An says, "Little damage?" The doctor explains that oxygen is dangerous for preemies given their underdeveloped lungs. Too much oxygen can dilate the blood vessels, detach retinas. An says, a bit impatiently, "I've always suspected oxygen of getting off easy. Sure, we blame greenhouse gases, but maybe it's the oxygen killing us all." Dr. Amelios looks perplexed. Jacob looks embarrassed. For the third time in three days, Jacob says, "An, it's not your fault." She snaps, "I never thought it was." She's getting the paranoid feeling that he's

26

speaking ironically, that he's secretly angry with her for belly-flopping in his gene pool. She stalks off to the vending machine to buy more peanut-butter cups.

At 24 weeks, a newborn's chances of survival are 70%. Severe disabilities occur at a rate of 20%. At 23 weeks, survival drops to 40% and disabilities jump to 60%. An tries memorizing these figures the way she once studied for math tests. She thinks: Which is older? A baby born at 23 weeks who's lived two-and-a-half weeks out of the womb? Or a baby delivered three days ago at 25 weeks? Sitting in her plastic chair, she watches a nurse spread Vaseline goo on a baby's skin to keep it moist. Across from An, Joey is being fitted with a breathing apparatus that resembles scuba gear. It's called a C-PAP. An tries to recall what the letters stand for; if she can just figure out this acronym everything will be fine. Her head is a playpen strewn with new words. Extremely premature babies are called micro-preemies: a fusion of science talk and baby talk. Micro-peepee, micro-poopoo. The incubators here are called iso-lettes. Then there's the litany of new words An has learned for what can go wrong: bradycardia, apnea, bronchopulmonary dysplasia, desatting, spastic diplegia, tracheotomy, retinopathy of prematurity.

Jacob brings An a *caffe latte* from a nearby coffee shop. With her hands wrapped around the warm Styrofoam cup, she mutters, "I don't want this." Jacob replies that it's decaf. "The bells and whistles, the tubes, the deadly oxygen," An says. "I don't want any of this." Jacob sighs, looks up at the fluorescent lights, looks down at B, who's wearing a mask over her eyes, like those that flight attendants hand out to passengers. Jacob mumbles, "She'll die without them." An says calmly, "If my womb rejected her, maybe she was meant to." As a child, she'd thought people were saying "youth in Asia": she'd pictured newborn Chinese girls swaddled in blankets and left on mountainsides to die.

An's mother is entertaining the troops. That's how An sees it. Lise is standing in the middle of NICK U with the other parents crowded around. They recognized her, of course. Her presence here is lucky, they must think. In the seventies, Lise played the Black Mouse in the children's television show *Les Souris dansent*. The part became her bête noire because, when the show ended, she struggled to get acting jobs in programs for adults. Lise is telling the parents about a miscarriage she had in her late thirties. An, her two younger sisters and her parents had been driving through Chicoutimi when her mother started bleeding. "After I lost the baby, I couldn't stop crying," Lise says. "The nurse wheeled me back to the waiting-room, took a look at my three little girls and said, 'Why all the fuss? You don't have enough kids as it is?'" The parents tsk-tsk, and Sheila touches Lise's arm in commiseration. An recalls that, when her mother was pregnant, she'd flick the heads of dandelions into An's face and say, "Mommy had a baby and her head popped off." Now An looks at her mother, wet-eyed and basking in the attention. She was a good mother, An thinks. She really was. Though at times, when Lise played with An and her sisters, dressed them all up in wigs and costumes for Little Red Riding Hood or Heidi, An had the uneasy feeling her mother was rehearsing for a part.

The blue espresso cup, the one Jacob had masturbated into, sat on the concrete wall of An's balcony. By this time, An was two months pregnant, already spitting up every morning in the kitchen sink. Jacob decided that, for luck, they had to break the cup. Toss it ten storeys to smash in the parking-lot below. They were talking about parenthood, and Jacob was describing his own parents, who lived out west. His father was a constant complainer prone to tantrums. When he'd discovered Jacob's stash of stolen Barbie dolls, he took them to his tool shed and decapitated them. "I remember screaming at him to at least spare the black one. She was unique—she was Afro Barbie." An mentioned her own parents, how her father and mother were so much in love they still took bubble baths together, with scented candles atop the toilet tank. Jacob joked, "Their profound love has set expectations that no boyfriend of yours can match." An replied, "Thank you, Dr. Kitchensink," and then pushed the blue cup off the edge.

An is telling B about Jacob. She talks about his feigned cynicism, his pretence at unconventionality with his dyed blue-black hair, the lizard tattooed on his hipbone. He's threatened to spike the lounge's water cooler with Ecstasy. Play some trance music over the PA system. A rave in NICK U! Strung-out fathers unfrazzled. Moms dancing with their kids' ventilators. "But really, B, Jacob is more dewy-eyed than my sisters and girlfriends. On an errand to pick up his dry cleaning, he'll fall in love twice." The unconventional one, An admits, is herself. "I don't fall in love, but I do fall in *like*. I could probably fall deeply in like." She looks at B's face, distorted by the air tube jammed into her mouth. She recalls Jacob kidding with her mother, asking why the French language doesn't distinguish between like and love. Why *aimer* is enough. Lise said that, for French people, to like is to love. "What do you think, B?" An asks her baby. She sticks a hand through the porthole and, with her index finger, touches B's elbow.

When An opens the front door to her apartment, she still smells taupe. That's the colour she painted her bedroom two weeks earlier. In the entrance hall are the bags of baby-shower gifts she got the night her contractions started. Sticking out the top of one bag is Mr. Pinkelton's malicious clown face. Her fantasy of tossing the gifts down the garbage chute is interrupted by the phone. She doesn't answer. All week she's spent talking to friends and family, repeating to everyone her Cole Porter refrain: "It's just one of those things." On her balcony, she pops open a bottle of Cabernet Sauvignon, thinking that at least now she can drink. As she sips, she sees the greenhouses atop McGill University's agriculture building a few blocks away. All that greenery so far off the ground is miraculous and consoling. In the apartment tower kitty-corner from hers, a woman carries a chair onto her balcony and steps onto it. For a dizzying instant, An thinks she's going to jump, but the woman simply hangs a pot of ivy.

An walks back to the hospital. The sun beats hot on her head. She's still dabbing sweat from her forehead as she enters the Pattycake Lounge. There, Sheila lurches out of her seat and flings herself at An. An feels the drag of the woman's weight, her body heat; she smells the oiliness of Sheila's scalp. Sheila begins sobbing, the sound resembling Mr. Pinkelton's phlegmy cough. An tries to pat the woman's back and pull away at the same time. "Joey?" An asks.

Jacob is in a private room down the hall from NICK U, in a plastic chair, cradling B in a tiny handmade quilt of green and yellow squares. Only B's face is visible. An sees that, without the air tube, the baby's mouth has the same rosebud lips as Jacob. He is singing now. Softly, slowly, as if his song were a lullaby, singing about the biggest word he's ever heard. She chose him as the father, thinking he wouldn't get attached. Yet here he is—cradling and crooning to his daughter. An sits on a trundle bed next to him. She fingers the quilt. The hospital gives these to parents as mementos: quilts and locks of hair and footprints of their dead babies. She wonders if, under the quilt, B's feet are already black with ink. Jacob says, "Would you like to hold her?" But An simply touches B's head, the soft spot where you can feel a baby's heartbeat but where she feels nothing. Jacob resumes his song, almost in a whisper now. An stares at B in his arms; she recalls the baby pushing everyone away in the delivery-room. After a moment, she says, "I don't love you." She waits for Jacob's usual "I don't love you, too," but when he looks at her, his face is ashen. He has understood what she meant. "Why?" he says, with a look of pain and puzzlement. "Oh, but I liked her," An says, almost pleadingly. "I liked her so much." Jacob starts crying. Soundlessly. When he finishes, he murmurs, "Well, that's something." And An, her arms wrapped around herself, holding herself together, hopes that it is.

Green Fluorescent Protein

The human genome is what Ruby-Doo is babbling about. The two of us are in Westmount Park. I'm practising my hook shots as he slumps on a bench alongside the basketball court.

Ruby-Doo has, what else, a book in his hands. He's a shortish, skinnyish guy. Well, at least compared with me.

"Wouldn't it be incredible," he says, scratching his armpit, "to map the thousands of genes in your body? Track down where each one comes from. Discover hidden traits."

Yesterday, his mother told me Ruby-Doo is a gifted child. But isn't gifted *child* an insult at seventeen? I'm seventeen too. One of my biggest gifts: twirling a b-ball on my index finger.

I sink the ball from half-court, and Ruby-Doo does the fake crowd roar—the hushed wahhhh—I taught him. I dribble over to his bench.

"Say you harbour the gene to become a musical prodigy," he says, blinking in the July sun. "Except you're totally unaware because you've never sat down at a piano. Unlike dwarfism or red hair, musical genius isn't visible. You see it only under special conditions."

In a field beside the courts, a theatre troupe is rehearsing *Romeo and Juliet*. Every now and then, Ruby-Doo is drowned out by some goof in tights yelling "Prodigious birth of love it is to me!" or something equally lame. But Ruby-Doo doesn't seem to notice; he rattles on about certain genes being top-secret files we need special security clearance to open. I remember my mom saying that alcoholism is hereditary and that maybe she and I both have the gene, so I tell Ruby-Doo I don't want to open those secret files.

"Probably bad news," I say.

Ruby-Doo eyes me like he's working on a science report on today's average teenager. "You know, Hippie," he says, "sometimes you're a real naysayer."

What the hell's a naysayer?

"Piss off," I say.

My real name is Max. Hippie is what Ruby-Doo calls me. The nickname is a joke: I have a buzz cut, wear polo shirts with little alligator logos and play on a basketball team. I call René-Louis Robidoux by his last name, pronouncing it like Scooby-Doo. We met at the start of the summer when my mom and I moved to Westmount from Saint-Bruno.

Every afternoon while I was shooting baskets, Ruby-Doo would be in the park reading. He always looked so absorbed; it bugged me. One day, I deliberately shot the ball at him, knocking his book flying.

Apologizing, I went and picked up the book and dusted it off. On the cover was the whiskered mug of a monkey. "What's your book about?" I asked, handing it over.

The Third Chimpanzee, he said, was about evolution and genetics, about the development of language and art.

"And also about sexuality," he added.

"Sexuality?"

"Yeah, like why women can't tell when they're ovulating," he said, straight-faced. "Like why men have such long dicks but such small balls compared with chimps."

I held the b-ball to my hip.

"You're kidding, right?"

His mouth curled into a grin. That's when I noticed his eyes: one was brownish, the other blue. Just like some Alaskan huskies you see.

My mom and I moved to Westmount as part of her Life Overhaul. She wanted everything new. New job: as a partner in a private dermatology clinic. New boyfriend: a dweeb anaesthesiologist named Brian who calls me Sport and sucks on toothpicks in public. New hair dye: something called Peruvian Fire (looks like the colour of barbecue chips). New AA group: the Westmount chapter, which she goes to every week.

Our new home is the top floor of this big brick house around the corner from the YMCA. The apartment has a wicked long hallway, like a bowling alley of blond wood. Another cool thing: the private bathroom off my bedroom has a fancy stained-glass window that makes taking a leak a religious experience.

One night, I get home from Passion des Fruits—the grocery store where I stack produce part-time—and find my mom sprucing up for a date. She frowns at herself in a hallway mirror. "These canine teeth of mine," she says, "stick out like box seats at the opera."

While poking in her clunky earrings, she asks whether Brian reminds me of my dad: "You know, the bear chest, the pointy chin."

"Maybe," I say. "Except Brian isn't some dead stiff whose widow is already screwing around."

My mom turns the colour of her hair. "You little shit," she spits out. "Don't you tell me how to grieve."

"Ma, I'm only joking," I lie.

She throws an earring at me. Misses me by a mile.

Two years and two months ago, my dad died of a brain aneurysm. Just dropped dead on the curling rink while lining up a shot. He was a big curler, my dad. He once joked he'd like his ashes placed in a hollowed-out curling stone.

Guess what—my mom decided to do it.

"For cripe's sake, he was only kidding!" I shouted and then burst into these weird yelping sobs. My mom grabbed me by the shoulders, pressing so hard my tears instantly stopped. "Listen to me, Max," she said in a freaky yell-whisper. "We all need a little levity. You understand me?"

34

I didn't argue. I didn't want to stress her out even more because in times of stress, she'd often drop in on her old cronies Margarita and Bloody Mary. Two weeks after the funeral, I found her in the kitchen, pale and shaky. In her hands was a two-arm corkscrew contraption, like something you'd abort a fetus with.

"Whatcha doing, Ma?" My voice sounded small and babyish. Scared.

"Nothing, honey," she mumbled.

That's when I saw the bottle of white wine on the counter. I stood in the doorway, watching her uncork her bottle, pour a glass, and dump the rest—*clug, clug, clug*—down the sink. Then she held her glass up, stuck her nose inside...and just sniffed!

As she shuffled out of the kitchen, she handed me the glass of wine. I took a sip of the stuff—it tasted like liquid headache—and then poured the rest into a vase of wilting funeral flowers.

"Remarkable," Ruby-Doo says when he sees the curling stone sitting on my mom's desk like some mammoth paperweight.

"Can I pick it up?"

I nod, and he lifts the stone gently by its curved handle and sits with it in a leather armchair. He rubs his palm over the stone's granite surface, which is bluish grey with these flecks of white.

Till Ruby-Doo, I've told none of my friends about the curling stone: it's sort of moronic having your dad stopped up like a cremated genie in a bottle.

"Tell me about your father," Ruby-Doo says.

So I sit down on my mom's bed and talk about my dad. How he was an English lit prof at CEGEP. How in front of my friends, he used expressions like "gee willickers" and "jiminy cricket" just to mortify me.

"Tell me more, Hippie," Ruby-Doo keeps saying. So I

keep tripping down memory lane, dodging a few potholes, like how miserable my mom's drinking made my dad.

"His voice," I say, "was a real tw*aaangy* drawl 'cause he grew up in Alab*aaama*. And what a motormouth—he was always blabbing away. I'd fade him out like Muzak. But after he died, our house got dead quiet, so I guess I kind of missed the background noise of his voice."

Usually I don't tell people super-confidential things like this. But I do with Ruby-Doo, and I swear he gets all teary-eyed. For a couple seconds, I feel the same awful pain I felt when my dad died—like having shin splints in your heart. But then I glance over at Ruby-Doo and burst out laughing.

"What?" he says. "What's so funny?"

The guy is cradling and petting the curling stone like a frigging pussycat. I take the stone from him and put it back on the desk. Then I pick Ruby-Doo up—he's as light as a girl—and throw him on my mom's bed.

"Hey," he says. "Hey!"

From the living-room, my mom yells, "No rough-housing," like we're ten years old.

Ruby-Doo's house is big and dark and crammed with old uncomfortable furniture with claw feet. On the walls are these gloomy sepia photographs of dead relatives.

He's invited me over for his parents' backyard barbecue. I'm expecting hotdogs and hamburgers, but the party is catered. Waiters carrying trays of dinky hors d'oeuvres snake through a crowd of guests. There are men in linen suits and bow ties. There's a woman hired to play violin. Apart from two six-year-old brats who keep winging a Frisbee at the violinist, I'm the youngest person here.

For some privacy, Ruby-Doo and I eat our dessert—sugar pie—on his screened-in verandah. He's jabbering on about this freakazoid named Nicholas Pop, an American artist who transfers genes between species.

"The guy has isolated the green fluorescent protein that makes the Pacific Northwest jellyfish glow," Ruby-Doo says, waving his fork. "And get this: he's injected that gene into the zygote of a guinea pig. Straight into its DNA."

His face lights up and his left knee jiggles as he talks. Watching him, I realize how bizarre my old Saint-Bruno friends would consider Ruby-Doo.

"Under regular light, the animal looks normal—just an albino guinea pig. But add some ultraviolet light and the thing glows an eerie fluorescent green."

"Why call this quack an artist?" I ask. "Is a glow-in-the-dark rodent art?"

"Depends," Ruby-Doo mumbles, his mouth packed with pie. He swallows loudly. "What if art is finding beauty in unexpected places?"

This Pop guy has a website: www.chimera.com. Ruby-Doo e-mailed him a sort of fan letter and Pop replied. Seems Pop will be lecturing in Montreal soon and has sent Ruby-Doo two free tickets. Ruby-Doo pulls the tickets from his pocket and hands me one.

"For you, Hippie," he says, patting my knee. "To thank you for listening to my deranged rambling."

The ticket is fluorescent green. On one side is the date of the lecture, along with the address of the theatre. On the other side is one word, which I say out loud: "Glow."

Us eating out, my mom jokes, is how my dad would want his insurance money spent. So every Thursday night, we go to a new restaurant—Indian, Ethiopian, Thai, Mexican, whatever—and try ordering something we don't usually put in our mouths. Tonight, I polish off fava-bean chowder and quail stuffed with apples and thyme; my mom downs escargot with goat cheese and then a bowl of oysters. We're in this homey French place with a dozen tables. Ours is covered in a yellow tablecloth decorated in a pattern of sunflowers and what look like dung beetles.

While I check out the dessert menu, my mom asks how I'm enjoying my summer job.

"I stacked a tub of eggplants today," I say. "Ever notice how beautiful they are? With their little purple bellies like Buddha."

I'm trying to find beauty in unexpected places, but my mother just looks at me funny. "What's happened to my son, the Jock Philistine?" she says.

"The Jock Philistine" is what my old girlfriend, Madison O'Connor, used to call me. Even in front of my mom.

"Heard from Madison lately?" my mom asks, and I shake my head.

Madison wore perfume that smelled like that strawberry powder you mix in milk. After she moved to Chicago, I bought a can of the stuff to remember her by. But by the time I'd finished the can, we'd more or less stopped writing each other.

"Some relationships just fizzle out," my mom says and sighs real dramatically like she's in a play.

"Okay—what's up?"

She plays origami with her napkin a bit. Then blurts out: "Brian proposed to me."

The quail I ate is suddenly pecking its way through my gut.

"I'm going to say no," she says, seeing my stunned look. "We've only been dating four months." She rummages her hands through her hair. "Brian is lovely, but he's...a tad boring. I mean, the man's the only anaesthesiologist who doesn't need drugs to put a person to sleep."

She laughs at her joke, her trademark guffaw that flashes the fillings in her teeth.

I feel guilty having hassled her about Brian. "You dating," I say, "I think it's a good thing."

My mom raises her eyebrows at me.

"No, I really do," I say and wonder if it's the truth. Then I say what I know is the truth: "Dad would want you to."

I feel sort of bad bringing my father up, but my mom just smiles down at her empty oyster shells, her bowl of castanets.

That night, I overhear my mom talking in her room with the door shut. She says, "One thousand days of sobriety." I assume she's on the phone with one of her batty friends, till she adds, "Can you believe it, Carl?"

She's talking to the curling stone.

On Friday, I have the day off from the grocery store. Around noon, our door buzzer buzzes. When I press the intercom, I hear Ruby-Doo's crackly voice whining, "Can Max come out and play?"

He takes me on a tour of some of his favourite sights in Montreal. Outside Square Victoria metro station, he points out these street lamps: two curvy, lizard-green monstrosities with piss-yellow eyes. They're extraterrestrials attacking a suburban town in a horror flick from the fifties. In a nearby building, we ride his favourite elevator: a birdcage-like contraption operated by a dandruffy old geezer. All the way up, this guy announces the floors in a bilingual garble: "twauziemturdfloor...katriemfortfloor."

Later, we walk down a snaky street where cobblestones poke through the asphalt. Sandwiched between two brick triplexes is this tiny wooden house Ruby-Doo wants to show me. It's caramel-coloured and has big shutters and a shingled roof. If we rang the bell, the door would be answered by Hansel and Gretel.

Farther down the street is a little park with a cement statue of a curled-up dog taking a snooze. Ruby-Doo pats the dog's head and says, "What about you, Hippie? What sorts of things do you love?"

Nothing leaps to mind, so I say, "Taking walks with my retarded friend," and Ruby-Doo beams me this sunny smile like I've given him a supreme compliment.

Around suppertime, we wander through the downtown core. The streets are closed off for the jazz festival, and hundreds of people are milling around. A stage is set up in front of the art museum. We find an empty stretch of grass on the museum's lawn and plunk ourselves down. Sitting nearby are two punks: a purple-haired guy and a blue-haired girl, both with shaved eyebrows. Ruby-Doo points out the pet rat Blue Hair has perched on her shoulder. "You think you're special, Hippie," he says. "But dismantle your genome and you'll find you have the same building blocks as that rat."

I'm about to say, *I don't think I'm special,* but stop myself because the day has been one of those perfect days that have you believing you *are* something special.

Ruby-Doo says the rat and I have been put together with the same deluxe set of Legos. "What differs," he says, "is the pieces chosen and the order they're stacked in."

Up on stage, a singer vacuum-packed into a tight dress slinks over to the mike. I lie back in the grass and listen to her low, gravelly voice sing about love and loss and Ruby-Doo's high, cheery voice talk about life and Legos.

We play two-on-one: me against Ruby-Doo and the nurse from *Romeo and Juliet.* The nurse's name is Charlotte, a pretty, twenty-year-old girl who probably didn't get cast as Juliet because she's black and fat.

"Get your skinny butt moving," she yells at Ruby-Doo, lobbing him the ball.

He looks at her in amazement. By the time Charlotte is called back to rehearsal, Ruby-Doo's T-shirt is spotted with sweat like those ink-blot tests shrinks use. He falls down on the court. "No more," he huffs. "God have mercy on my skinny white butt."

We head back to my place to eat supper and watch his favourite movie, *2001: A Space Odyssey.* My mom is in the kitchen stirring a wooden spoon in a pot on the stove.

"Salut, Max. Salut, Ruby-Doo," she says. "Je vous fais du chili ce soir, les gars."

This bugs me for two reasons. First, only I get to call René-Louis Ruby-Doo. Second, why does my mom always humiliate me with her crappy French?

My mom scoops out some chili and holds the spoon to Ruby-Doo's lips. "Délicieux," he mumbles. Some sauce has smudged on his chin, and my mom wipes it off with a dish towel, slinging an arm across his shoulder. Then she ruffles his hair. My mom has always been touchy-feely, which can be mortifyingly embarrassing.

Ruby-Doo looks at her shyly. "Want to watch the movie with us, Peggy?"

Peggy says she can't because she's leaving in five minutes for AA.

Peggy says AA like it was PTA.

Ruby-Doo looks a bit flustered. "Oh, okay," he says. "Hey, I'm sorry."

"No need to be," my mom insists. "My drinking has been under control for years." Then: "You're surprised because I'm a doctor."

"No, no," he says.

"Some MDs even drink on the job," my mom says. "The oath they take is hypocritical rather than Hippocratic." She does her usual guffaw.

As I pour us glasses of water, Ruby-Doo says in his Mr. Science mode that he's read alcoholism is a disease.

More like a self-inflicted wound, I think. My mom once picked me up from Cub Scouts totally plastered. After that, the scout leader always asked how my "home life" was like he was all eager to call Children's Aid.

As my mom natters on, I announce that Ruby-Doo has to take his shower. Once he's gone off to my room, my mom turns to me: "Does my alcoholism still embarrass you?" She jabs her wooden spoon at me. "I've learned to accept it, and so should you."

Sounds like step eight of her twelve-step program.

"Look, what embarrasses me," I say, "is you pawing Ruby-Doo." To be nasty, I add, "Aren't you too old for him?"

She looks straight at me: "You jealous?"

As if I'd be jealous of Ruby-Doo.

After my mom is gone, I peel off my sweaty T-shirt and push open the door to my room. Puddly footprints trail from my bathroom to my dresser. Ruby-Doo stands at the dresser mirror raking a comb across his head. At his feet is his duffel bag with a tumble of clothes hanging out.

I walk up behind him. One of my beach towels circles his waist, and water beads on his back. On the nape of his neck are these little blond hairs.

"So is skinny-ass all clean?" I say. As a joke, I yank his towel off. I'm going to say, *Yep, sure is skinny*, but with him there naked, the words get trapped behind my teeth.

In the mirror, Ruby-Doo is watching me, his pupils the size of pennies. We stare at each other like it's a staring contest, so I feel like the loser when I blink and look away.

He lies his comb down and turns slowly around. I see his blue eye first, then his brown eye. He reaches up, cups a hand around my left biceps.

He squeezes.

I pull away.

"Shower time," I mumble. I hurry into the bathroom, locking the door.

The shower I take is long and cool, but somehow I'm still sweating after I switch off the taps.

During the opening scene, an ape-man swings a club and crushes the skull of a wild boar.

On opposite ends of the couch, Ruby-Doo and I sit watching *2001*. His voice cracking like a thirteen-year-old puberty case, Ruby-Doo says, "It's good your mom

42

goes to AA."

I say, "Uh-huh." I keep my eyes glued to the TV screen and spoon chili into my mouth.

In another scene, a spacecraft flies to the moon. On board is a stewardess who wears shoes with Velcro soles to anchor her to the floor.

Later, when Ruby-Doo finally leaves, I walk around our apartment like that stewardess. Taking careful, measured steps so I don't float off into zero gravity.

For the next few days, Ruby-Doo is in Quebec City attending his older sister's wedding. I stack Swiss chard and bok choy; I stack tangerines and mangoes.

I call up Pete, an old friend from Saint-Bruno, and we go skating on the bike paths that criss-cross the Plateau. Pete is tall and gangly; he has red hair and a smattering of freckles. With Rollerblades on, he's a giraffe on wheels.

We buy hotdogs blanketed in sauerkraut and wolf them down sitting on a stoop outside a french-fry place. Pete nudges me and nods toward two girls sitting nearby. He whispers, "Eager beavers," his expression for girls on the make.

I look over at the girls. Then I look past them, down a back lane where every duplex has an outdoor spiral staircase twisting from the ground to the top balcony.

During our walking tour, Ruby-Doo compared Montreal's spiral staircases to DNA.

I wonder what he's doing at this exact moment. What he's thinking about. Then I realize it's damn faggy to wonder these things and that I'd better snap out of it.

So I go talk to the girls with Pete. I make jokes. I flash a big cheesy smile. To show off, I do a handstand with my skates on. With my T-shirt riding up, the blood pooling in my head, the hotdog somersaulting in my stomach, I almost feel normal.

Last year, I'm at this party thrown by this guy Charlie Deller, a basketball player from another school. At one point, Charlie takes me into his dad's study. At the wet bar, he pours us glasses of crème de menthe, which tastes like concentrated mouthwash. Charlie is a little drunk. One minute he's bragging about bench-pressing 180; next minute he leans over and licks my cheek like it's a frigging ice-cream cone. "You've got nice skin," he says just before his girlfriend walks in.

A week later, our b-ball team plays his. Charlie Deller sees me, says, "Hey man, how's it going?" All nonchalant like it isn't queer for people to go around licking faces.

Charlie decides to ignore what happened. Pretty smart move because now whenever I bump into him, I practically think I dreamed the whole cheek-licking episode up.

Saturday afternoon, I'm in the park, slam-dunking a few when Ruby-Doo rides up on his clunky bicycle, a knapsack strapped to his back. I go over to say hi, hugging the b-ball to my stomach; I ask how the wedding was.

"Stuffy. Overblown," he says. "It made me want to live in sin."

Ruby-Doo smiles, and I feel creepy, like maybe he's implying *we* should live in sin. So I look down at a little sandy anthill spilling out of a crack in the concrete. I smudge the anthill with my foot.

Ruby-Doo opens the drawstring of his knapsack and yanks out a big box wrapped in aluminum foil. "For you," he says, handing it over.

I stand there staring at the box, my throat as dry as a tortilla chip.

"Well, go ahead and open it." He rubs his palms on his jeans like he's wiping away sweat.

I unpeel the foil. It's a shoebox. Inside are Riko basketball sneakers. Fire-hydrant-red stripes and air-bubble soles. Tongues sticking out at me.

"It's not my birthday."

"So what," Ruby-Doo says. "Try them on. You take nine and a half, right?"

I sit on the bench, wriggle my old sneakers off, and lace the Rikos up. Then I boing up and down the court, thinking, *So he bought you a gift. Means nothing.*

"Perfect fit," I say.

"Look at you," Ruby-Doo shouts with a big smile. "Cinderella of the basketball court."

I glare at him: "What'd you call me?"

"What?" he says.

In the pissed-off yell-whisper my mom uses on me, I snap, "I'm no Cinderella, okay."

"Okay, okay," Ruby-Doo replies. Then a sly look flits across his face. "But you got to admit," he says, "when it comes to princes, I'm pretty charming."

My anger stings like a rug burn.

I rip the left Riko off and throw it on the ground. The right Riko I whip across the court at Ruby-Doo's head, smacking him hard in the face.

He flinches. Cups a hand over his nose.

I just stand there, embarrassed. Like a ten-year-old who's had a tantrum in public.

Ruby-Doo draws his hand away. I expect blood, but there's none. Still, his nose is blotchy and his eyes are red and teary.

He walks toward me.

I look down at my stocking feet; I expect him to punch me and I hope he does. But he brushes past, his shoulder skimming mine. Under his breath, he mutters, "You're welcome."

When I get home, I shove the Rikos under my bed with my old puzzles and dinosaur models and sports trophies.

Nauseous and dizzy—that's how I feel. Like my organs —heart, stomach, pituitary gland—are strapped into a

Rotowhirl at the midway.

I lie on my bed.

I try to think. I try to stay calm. I try to be logical.

Okay, proof I'm not queer: I did it with Madison once. So what if it wasn't that romantic. We had a bath together first and she'd poured in tons of bubble-bath powder. Well, the stuff left a gross soapy film on our skin. Still all my parts worked the way they're supposed to. The whole time I kept thinking we were performing some weird calisthenics for gym class.

I think, *Do I want to do calisthenics with Ruby-Doo?*

Then I feel totally disgusted. At myself for hurting Ruby-Doo. At Ruby-Doo for calling me his princess.

And especially at myself for wanting to hold Ruby-Doo after I hurt him.

Later there's a knock on my bedroom door.

"Go away!" I yell at my mom.

She comes in anyway, spritzing her neck with eau de toilette and wearing a blouse that looks like the stuff they make doilies out of. She flushed Brian last week and already has a coffee date with some chatroom conquest she met on the Internet.

"How do I look?"

I lie that she has too much lipstick on, and she kisses a Kleenex to blot her mouth.

"I hope you know," I say, "that women are entrapped on the Net and sold into white slavery."

Picking invisible lint from her skirt, she says, "Sometimes, Max, you got to be willing to take such chances."

I want to say, *Don't go.* Not that I'm afraid her date is an axe murderer. Or that I don't want her meeting someone, getting over my father. Or even that I want to talk about what's eating me. I'd just like her here, that's all. Putzing around the apartment the way moms do while I sulk in my room.

She bends down, kisses my forehead. "You still going out with René-Louis tonight?" she asks.

I shrug. That lecture with the damn glow-in-the-dark rodent is at seven o'clock. My green fluorescent ticket is thumbtacked to my bulletin board.

After my mom leaves, I pour myself some Cheerios for supper. But my appetite is shot, so I leave the little life preservers floating in their milk.

I pace around the apartment. Drift from room to room. I end up in my mom's room, flipping through *Romeo and Juliet*, which I spot on her bookshelf. It's my dad's class-room copy, all dog-eared and mangled. In the margins, he's pencilled in his comments.

"Love isn't a play on words," he's written in Act II. "Rather it's words at play, let out at recess to go swing on the monkey bars."

What the fuck does that mean?

Suddenly I'm furious with my dad for being so frigging cryptic, for not being here to set me straight. For being stone-cold dead.

I grab up the curling stone and go into our bowling-alley hallway. I slide that sucker down the hall with such force it smacks against the back wall, nicking the paint and leaving a monster dent.

I sit on the floor.

I jab the tips of my index fingers into the corners of my eyes to stop myself from bawling.

It doesn't work.

Once, when I was thirteen, I saw my dad cry.

We were staying at our cottage on Danforth Lake. I'd been off picking raspberries. When I got back, I could hear my mom's voice: loud and gin-and-tonicky. She was on the patio with the German couple from the cottage next door.

When she saw me, she screeched, "There's my baby!"

To get away from her, I went down to the dock. My dad

was sitting there, his feet dangling in the water. I snuck up, hoping to scare him. But before I could yell "Raahh!" the dock creaked and my dad turned his head.

His cheeks were wet, his eyes bloodshot. Snot was rolling out of his nose.

I was terrified.

Still I sat down beside him, dunked my feet in the water, and watched tadpoles as big as kiwi fruit nibble at my toes.

"You hate her, don't you?" I finally said. "You hate her guts."

"No, Max," he said, wiping the snot with the back of his hand. "I was crying because I love her guts."

It's 7.30 by the time I reach Ex-Centris, the theatre where Nicholas Pop is giving his talk on glowing rodents. Out front, a dozen picketers are traipsing up and down the sidewalk. They wear green glow-in-the-dark necklaces and wave placards: BRILLER, C'EST PAS BRILLANT! and REMEMBER DR. FRANKENSTEIN!

The beefy guy at the door doesn't want to let me in, but when I whip out my ticket, he sweeps me through. Ex-Centris is one long lobby with a stone floor and a glass ceiling. Off the lobby are three rooms. The ticket girl says I'm late and points me toward the Salle Fellini.

I slink inside this low-lit hall where a guy dressed in black is on stage talking. Scanning the audience—there must be 200 people here—I finally spot the back of Ruby-Doo's head near the front.

As I'm wedging into the second row, the guy on stage—Pop, I guess—says, "I don't care about aesthetics. Aesthetics to me is what primatology is to monkeys." The audience starts laughing; so does Ruby-Doo, till he sees me toddling toward him. After stepping my Rikos on seventeen feet, I shoehorn myself into the empty seat beside him.

"Hi," I whisper.

"Well, if it ain't Cinderella's ugly stepsister," he mutters, looking straight ahead.

"Yeah," I say.

There's a chalky taste, like a dissolved Aspirin, in my mouth. I turn and face the stage. That's when I notice the albino guinea pig. It's inside a see-through plastic hutch set on a table near Pop.

"Man has tinkered with the evolution of plants and animals for thousands of years. So creating hybrids violates no social precedence," Pop says, his voice booming through some hidden mike. The guy is a preacher with a rock star's goatee and leather pants. He talks on about jellyfish and mutation and enzymes while a screen behind him flashes images of Petri dishes, X and Y chromosomes, and whatnot.

I'm barely paying attention. Instead I listen to Ruby-Doo's breath going in and out. *Here's what you do*, I think. *Apologize. Tell him he's a great guy, a good friend—but just a friend. Then do a Charlie Deller and pretend nothing happened.*

Pop fishes his guinea pig out of its cage. Its hind legs pirouette as the guy tucks the animal to his chest. We're seated so close I can see the guinea pig's dark red eyes, which look like beads of blood.

"My aim with little Chimera," Pop says, petting the animal's white fur and pink petal ears, "is to challenge what we define as genetically pure. What we define as otherness."

The guinea pig squirms in Pop's arms, squeaking like a baby's squeeze toy.

"Green fluorescent protein," Pop says, "doesn't change the creature in any significant way but one."

Just then, angry shouts erupt in the lobby.

Pop's booming voice says, "But what tremendous importance we place on that one thing."

The theatre's back doors bang open, and we all swivel in our seats. The picketers march through, chanting, "Hell, no, we won't glow!" One protester tosses leaflets in the air. A woman in an aisle seat jumps up and tries wrestling away a placard, but she stumbles backward with a yelp into some guy's lap. Meanwhile, the beefy doorman storms in red-faced and growling, "Câlice de tabarnac!"

Ruby-Doo turns toward me, his left leg brushing against my right…and I swear I want to move away but my leg stays put.

"Bedlam," he says with a grin.

"Totally," I whisper.

Up on stage, Pop nods toward the projection-room. Off go all the house lights. For two seconds, pitch blackness. Then a loud click. Then a bluish shaft of light beaming down from the rafters.

In Pop's arms, the white guinea pig turns a brilliant green. Like crème de menthe. Like a traffic light telling you to go. Like the glowing skin of Frankenstein's monster.

It's very weird and really scary.

And kind of beautiful in an unexpected way.

MAUREEN BILERMAN

We drive two hours north. When we pull up to the Bed and Breakfast I resist saying it looks just like my parents' house. I'm a bit of a trouble-shooter. In the spirit of romance, I hold back the criticism and take personal renovation notes instead. For Sam's sake, I even mutter *Wow*—before continuing down my silent checklist. One new paint job—check; plastic fawn removal—check. We park in the driveway and I am surprised at how far back the house goes. I can read the history of the B&B—the good years and the bad—in the choppy extensions they've added on, like rings in a tree reveal age.

My kids have taught me about the toxic nature of expectation, and what could be more of a build-up then a lovers' retreat? But my husband and I need a break from the kids, so when my mother volunteers to take them for the night, we move fast before she comes to her senses.

Usually we'd go canoeing or fishing, but it's winter and although we could snowshoe into our camp, the truth is, we're too tired for adventure. Regardless, I couldn't resist flipping through the Outdoor Adventure Brochure in bed one night, hoping to muster enough reserve strength for a dog sledding trek. That's when I stumbled across the section on Romantic Getaways. The couple in the ad were curled up in front of a fireplace, faces glowing like butter. Even though I knew better, I was lulled by words like relaxing, rekindle and chocolate dipped. I flashed the ad under Sam's nose.

"Your choice," he said.

I hate deciding things like this. I remember the time I chose shopping at the Outlets in Maine. We spent one full day in L.L Beans combing through camping supplies, and the second day I sat on a wall eating ice cream, listening to Sam heckle parcel-toting Americans. It may have been my choice to shop, but it wasn't where he wanted to be. Besides I'm leery of choosing romance. Especially after driving the Cabot Trail together last summer. Pockets of silence lay in front of us like heat puddles on the highway. Always another one, just up ahead.

"You decide," I said, handing him the brochure.

Norma shows us to our room. She has a big smile on her face that is disconnected from her eyes. The kind of smile I've thrown on myself, when the kids are underfoot and I don't want them to know something is wrong. The room is raspberry red. If it is supposed to be sexy, it has been seriously undermined by the crocheted doilies on the wall, the brass fixtures, the slippery Sears bedspread.

I strengthen my resolve not to complain. But I feel like a reformed drinker walking into an open bar party. I'll need to keep my wits about me if I'm to resist slamming the place in one shot. Norma fluffs the pillows and opens the closet. She talks nonstop about the woman who originally booked the room for tonight, but never sent her deposit.

"I hope she shows up," Norma says, smiling harder.

She throws back the curtains to show us the outdoor hot tub. We follow her outside, her big thighs leaving a trail of polyester whispers.

After she leaves, Sam says, "Norma seems pretty nice." I say nothing. I think she should have *I hate people* cross-stitched on her ass—it's so obvious. Sam sees the best in everyone. Most of the time I'm grateful. But even optimism has its downside. It is after all, a happy rut.

He bounces once on the corner of the bed to test the mattress, than raises both eyebrows at me in approval. I don't know why I can't stand a come-on. It's getting worse with time. I used to laugh when he tweaked both my nipples in the standard *dialing Tokyo* grope. Now the sensation is irritating, reminds me of when I sloughed my nipples with a towel in preparation for breast-feeding. Sam tries to remember I'm sensitive to his sexual humour. Sometimes he even uses the marriage counsellor's suggested love-making pitch—verbatim. *Are you open to the possibility, tonight?* But we haven't been to counselling in a while and he's forgotten again, so I give him a raised eyebrow back and dive into the bowl of Hershey kisses on the table.

We poke around the room, sift through the basket of massage oils and lotions Norma has left for us. I catch Sam's eye and we both laugh.

"What now?" he asks.

I scan the indoor hot tub. There is a picture of a white fence painted along the wall beside it. Pansies wind themselves around the pickets at an impossible height. Funny it should be pansies. Pansies are a symbol of remembering, not very romantic at all.

"Let's go skiing," I say.

The weather is turning. Driving in the truck on the way to the cross-country ski trails, we listen to the weatherman. The rain is supposed to stop as temperatures drop to minus 30 by nightfall. There isn't much to see out the truck window. Just a few houses clustered along the highway, swing sets rusting in the snow. The drizzle is almost more than this place can bear.

I wonder if Sam has been thinking about our trip to Cape Breton too. The perfect Bed & Breakfast we stumbled across. When the owner left, we ran through the house like it was a palace; pine interior, top of the line pool table, fitness-room, jacuzzi. We had the whole place to ourselves. We'd been fighting three days straight in the car and hadn't made love in a month. Sam spent the evening fiddling with the satellite remote. I got through half my novel in the hot tub. Finally there was nothing left to do but go to bed.

"Stop," I said, five minutes into the foreplay.

In the beginning of our marriage, I would have kept going. But after six months of sex therapy, I had learned that disengaged love-making is a downward spiral. Sam knew this too, and the last thing he wanted was to end up back in therapy. Six months of abstaining from sex, six months of back tickles and massages and getting to know each other again. I didn't mind. It was like being on a weight gain diet. Diet without hunger. Except it was sex without the sex. When I said no in Cape Breton, Sam knew what was at stake, but he got mad just the same. Of course, he blamed it *on the way* I had said no. Whatever happened, it marked another new beginning in our marriage. He stopped asking me to make love.

There are no other cars in the parking-lot when we arrive at the ski trails. I jump down from the truck, and instantly know the wind is going to keep its Arctic promises. Inside the lodge, the caretaker is sitting by the fire hunched over a deck of cards. He refuses to look up when we walk in. I sign the guest book and we head back outside to grab our cross-country skis.

Mr. Solitaire hasn't bothered to groom the trails, so we follow old ski tracks fossilized in snow. The temperature continues to plummet, and a strange wind strums the tops of the pine trees; a haunting sound. The wind spills a thin glaze across the snow. Sam and I take turns breaking through. It's hard work and slow moving but at least we have the woods to ourselves.

I can hear Sam skiing behind me. He is over six feet tall and his long glides sound like pages being torn slowly from a book. I think of our travels, before we were married. The exotic love poems I ripped out of my journals to give him. Sam and I have visited some remote places on the planet; fed live goats to the Komodo dragons in Indonesia, floated into Laos on rubber tires, driven the rugged Oodnadatta track through the Aussie Outback. So I can say with some experience that marriage is a strange country. We would do better with a translator, a live-in marriage counsellor perhaps. Why not? People hire nannies as a buffer for their kids. I ski slowly and imagine Sam trying to steer away from issues, the way happy people always do. I imagine the counsellor intervening on my behalf from across the kitchen table.

"Sorry to interject, Sam, but Barb is the one with the initial issue, remember. You've just shifted the focus to yourself again. Go ahead, Barb."

Marriage is a strange country. The deeper we travel, the dimmer the flashlight.

I race ahead until I'm out of Sam's sight. I punch *I love you* in the snow with my ski pole where he's sure to see it. I reach the warming hut and pop my skis off. A few logs have been cut into chairs and set around the wood stove. There is no fire, but it feels cozy. Sam arrives and sits down beside me. We kiss. My hands cup his cold cheeks, his tongue pours like warm liquid into my mouth.

"This is perfect," I say.

When we get back to the Bed and Breakfast, Norma's daughter Louise is in the kitchen. She is 30-ish with dark eyes. She offers to cook us supper but we've already eaten on the way back through town. Louise tells us her mother is at the mall working a booth at the bridal show, even though she hates doing it.

A small child with black hair darts through the hallway.

"That's my daughter Rachel," Louise says.

Rachel inches down the hall, and when she reaches us she stomps past. She has a picture folded in her hand which she gives to Louise. *I can't get the heart right,* she hisses, trying hard not to look in our direction. Louise works it a bit with a red crayon and sends Rachel back to her room.

"She's making a Valentine's Day card for Mom and it has to be perfect," Louise says, rolling her eyes.

I nod in complete understanding. Imagine my own daughter wailing in frustration when something isn't *per-feck,* as she calls it. Whenever I start to correct her pronunciation, I resist. I think back to one of our marriage counselling sessions. Sam kept complaining that I was *condescending*, only he kept pronouncing it *con-den-sending*. If he'd only mispronounced it once, I would have been all right. But he kept repeating it. *That's con-de-sending*, I said slowly, knowing the session was about to turn in his favour.

Back up in our room, Sam clicks on the fireplace. It's not real. It's not even gas. It's a screen, and if you look close it is like sitting too near the television. The picture breaks down into a million tiny pieces. We lie in bed and I listen to the fireplace breathing. The vent is open, and there is the repetition of a long pull of air followed by a short one. I try and match my breathing to the sound, but I keep running out of breath.

Sam is stretched out beside me reading and making squeaky noises with his dental floss pick. Somewhere in the house I hear a drawer rolling on its track and landing with a muffled slam. It is a lonely sound. The ceiling fan is swirling overhead. My thoughts turn and turn.

Peter was my first love. He wore cowboy boots and carried a newspaper clipping in his breast pocket that said Peter's Flower Power Hour. It was two lines written up in the local paper about his high school radio show. He covered it in tape so it wouldn't rip when he showed it to everyone. Peter was three years older then I was. We waited over a year to have sex, trying to make it to my sixteenth birthday. Peter was still a virgin too. The closer my birthday got, the more we talked about it. The more we talked about it, the more determined he became.

When I finally said yes, he promised me a romantic night I would never forget when his parents left for Florida. By the next day it had become a special date *that* Saturday night. Only we never made it to the weekend. We raced home and did it during lunch hour, when my parents were at work.

Peter and I continued to do it every chance we got. At

first I thought maybe I was having orgasms and I didn't know it. But then I caught a look in Peter's eyes when he was coming, and wherever he went for those few seconds, I knew I had never been. One night when I was taking a bath, I let the water run between my legs. I kicked over a bottle of my dad's Head & Shoulders when I came. I couldn't wait to share my new discovery with Peter. I had thought I couldn't have an orgasm, and that there was something terribly wrong with me.

"I have a surprise for you," I said, on the phone.

Peter came over as soon as my parents were out. I pulled him into the bathroom and put the fuzzy toilet lid down so he would have a comfortable seat. He watched me strip with a baffled expression. Clambering into the tub, I adjusted the temperature, and hoisted my legs up carefully so I wouldn't take out all the hair products again. It wasn't until after my orgasm that I noticed the look on Peter's face. In all the excitement I had missed the transition from baffled to pissed off.

"Bitch," he said, on the way out.

Sam glances over from his book and spots the intensity on my face.

"What are you thinking about?" he asks.

I could tell him the truth. But I feel annoyed and I don't want to.

"I'm just wishing I could find one thing in this room I like," I say.

The complaint feels good coming out, warms me like a shot of liquor would, going in. Sam turns back to his book.

At bedtime, we make our way outside to the hot tub. Sam hops through the snow wrapped in a white robe and fluffy slippers. He is only a shower cap away from complete ridiculousness. He slides the lid of the whirlpool off and we lower ourselves in. Norma is right. I feel like I am a hot fudge sundae, except I'm hot on the bottom and cold on top. Snow blows off the roof and sprinkles my shoulders. Through the gaps in the gazebo roof, rows of stars are planted like seeds.

We soak beneath a tired light that hangs from the ceiling. Sam reads and I thumb an outdated People magazine Norma has left in the room, until my arms are too tired to hold the pages out of the water. I lay my head back against the tub and inhale the chlorine which is burning my vagina. The ph balance is off and the smell of bromine is overwhelming. Restless and unable to stand the pressure of looming sex any longer, I sidle up to Sam.

"Hey, you," he says, tossing his book on the chair.

He kisses me. I imagine just how many chemicals are in the water. I know where this could lead, Sam pushing chlorine deep into my body.

"I'm too hot in here," I whisper.

I motion my head toward the door leading back to the bedroom. He lifts his eyebrows a couple of times like Groucho Marx to make sure he's got my signal right. It's not as much fun getting out of the hot tub. My robe is covered in light snow. I scream when it touches my back.

Before we climb into bed, I unplug the angel standing guard on the end table. She looks like a tree-topper holding a light in each hand, but when I peek under her skirt, there is no hole for a tree. I stick her in the closet with the commemorative plate of Lady Diana I parked earlier. Satisfied, I crawl into bed.

Sam rolls over on his side and faces me.

"You smell like a rubber duck," I say.

He laughs and pinches my nipple playfully. *Too hard*, I say to myself. I feel my body start to rise like an elevator. Up, up, up to my head. I breathe deep and manage to ease my focus back to ground level, back to my body—where the action is. Then I catch the faint whiff of something under his breath and start analyzing the content. With every ingredient that gets silently ticked off, I move another inch away from the smorgasbord in Sam's mouth.

At some point I surrender and pleasure wins. I moan how good it feels. But to myself I am chanting, *It's okay to feel good, it's okay to feel good.* The brain loses. My body celebrates multiple victories. When it's over I'm relieved. It could have gone the other way, with my brain as champion, a clipped victory speech. My body forced to untangle itself prematurely from the fleshy pretzel of sex.

The next morning Norma serves us breakfast in the dining-room: yogurt, fruit, sausages and French toast. She tops up the coffee and the conversation every five minutes, chatting away about the guest who had her up for breakfast at seven this morning, and then didn't even leave until nine.

"Good thing he got me up so early," Norma says.

I leave a piece of my toast swimming in syrup on the plate. Norma clears it away.

"Something wrong with breakfast?" she asks with a smile.

Norma looks tired, her smile—a little weary, and I feel myself warm up to her a bit. She rattles on about the bridal show, how relieved she is that it's over.

"I'd rather be here," she says.

She waves her hand through the air. The dining-room is stuffed with trinkets. Porcelain dolls stand thigh high. The china cabinet is filled with pale blue figurines, doe-eyed children I recognize from Precious Moments greeting cards. I imagine Norma dusting each and every statue. When she tops my coffee up I ask her if she has cross-stitched the pictures on the wall herself.

"Hell no," she laughs. "I don't have enough patience. I just appreciate that someone does."

We pack slowly. I do the customary last check—flinging the bed skirt up, pulling the drawers open. *All set*, I say to Sam. He takes me by the hand and leads me into the bath-room. Climbing up on the closed toilet seat, he reaches his hand up to the top of the cabinet and pulls down a dusty pottery vase that I hadn't noticed.

"Do you like *this*?" he asks.

The vase is cream coloured with a green lip, just like my dishes at home.

"I do," I say.

I leave it on the end table where the angel was, in the hopes that Norma will take the hint and reconsider the room's décor. Sam looks at me softly until I put the vase back where it belongs in the bathroom. He leads me by the hand to the closet where I've hidden an array of Norma's ornaments.

Driving home, I twirl the stem of the chocolate rose Norma gave me on the way out. With my other hand, I tap a song on Sam's knee. It is Valentine's Day and CBC Radio is using love as a hook. I look out my window and see big red hearts pasted on storefronts.

"Why would they choose a heart to symbolize love?" I ask.

"Maybe it's the best they could come up with," Sam says.

"I could do better," I say.

I spend the rest of the trip entertaining Sam with my search for the perfect holiday symbol. In the end I settle on an old flashlight like the one we use at our camp. It never works right, but it never dies either. We just take turns tapping it back to life inside our palms.

Catch & Release

I'm prone to carsickness when Richard is behind the wheel. His personal mission statement includes exploring every back road in the province. Fast. It includes pee-breaks where he says he has to see a man about a horse, before heading to the back of the truck. I watch him sometimes through the passenger mirror, aiming at a large rock while the moose flies swarm inside the truck because he's left the door open. Again.

We pick up Luc on our way to the drop-off point. He owns some cabins and canoes in the area and charges $75 to ferry us to the headwaters. He is going to help us unload our canoe and gear before driving our truck to the mouth of the river. I sit on the console in the front seat of the truck between Luc and Richard. Luc is a big man with a black beard and moustache. If he worked at the newspaper I might be tempted to mention his body odour to a co-worker, but I lean into him in the truck for stability. He smells muddy and wild like a wet dog—so familiar, I ask him questions about his family.

"My mother was pregnant eighteen times," he says.

Richard catches air off a deep pocket in the road and I grab the dashboard to keep my head from hitting the roof.

"She's 86, had two children die and two miscarriages. It's harder on the men though. My father died fifteen years ago."

I feel saliva rise up the back of my throat. Force it down with a succession of hard swallows. I know that Richard is dying to hear Luc's stories, the ones that get passed between the fishermen he charters to the best pools on the river; men who talk of nothing but the sport. The more I steer the conversation away from that, the faster he drives. I suffer carsickness and if we were alone I'd insist he slow down, but I don't want to shatter Luc's rugged image of me. I give him a Yee-haw grin and swallow harder.

Richard pours a Perrier with a slice of lime and passes it
forward to me on the end of his paddle.

"For you, my Princess."

No even-Stephens on the river. We don't divide duties
the way we do so carefully at home. *Your turn to do lunches.*
My turn to be on top. Maybe it's the commitment of putting
in, of not being able to turn back, but our annual canoe trip
makes the relationship feel larger. There is, after all, plenty
of payback time. Whatever the reason, when Richard dotes
on me in the bush, I feel special. Liked, even. Last night,
while he filled our Italian rolls assembly-line fashion, he
shared the science and art of sandwich making with me. *The
two slices of Swiss cheese act as waterproof liners. Lettuce is next,
then meat, and always, always, the tomato in the centre, where it
does the least damage.*

We drift downriver. Letting everything outside of us, in.

A few hours later we stop to fish the pool in front of the
warden's station. It's still early in the season and the camp
is closed up. We cup our hands to the milky glass and peer
through cracks between the boards. Inside, there is a table
with only one chair. Looking in at the deserted camp my
chest feels hollow, and the sensation stays with me, linger-
ing like a boat in an eddy.

We run up the spiral stairs to the top of the lookout.

"Looklooklook," Richard says.

Hundreds of fish are running upriver in a steady line.

"Salmon?"

"If only," he says, and I nod, although we both know
that if salmon were that easy to hook we would be devastated.

We climb down the tower and cast our rods across the
river, but it's rough going. The water drops off too quickly
for us to wade, so we cast from the bottom of the bank. My
line keeps getting tangled in the trees behind me, wind ties

a knot in my leader, and even though a knot weakens the line by 50%, I leave it there, too frustrated to work it out. Richard laughs and throws another perfect roll cast.

We hear them before they arrive. Two canoes motoring upriver, stopping just short of us: it's Luc, a couple of sports, and another guide. You can tell the sports from the guides, same way you know a German when you travel Europe, they always have the best gear. The sports step out of an L.L Bean Catalogue. Tilley hats. Orvis rods. Luc is still wearing his old red-and-black checkered mackinaw.

"How's the fishing?" Luc asks Richard.

"Not great. The river's up."

They exchange information casually, carefully, the way fishermen do.

I can feel Luc checking me out from beneath his black felt hat, an arrhythmic stare, lasting one beat too long. I cast my line and miraculously the fly lands perfectly on the water.

"Your wife casts a nice line," Luc says.

I feel instantly guilty.

"I'm flirting with somebody at work," I said to Richard, just over a year ago, when the kids were finally in bed.

He nodded thoughtfully, as if I was answering some question he'd just been asking himself

"Has anything happened?"

"No," I answered, knowing full well he meant sex.

There was no point in telling him that sex was irrelevant.

"Lily-dipper," Richard says, once we're back on the river.

I use his taunt as an excuse to give up paddling and stretch my legs out over the gunwales of the canoe. River rocks get pulled from under me. The water casts an antique pallor on the stones, like old black-and-white photographs that have been retouched with colour: ivory, grey and salmon. No matter how hard I try, I won't recall a single stone at the end of the day.

I point to the silhouette of a moose. She must have moved or I would have missed her. Richard immediately gives his best call; one long wail, followed by two short grunts. It works better in the woods than it does in the bedroom. The moose startles, and from beneath the brown canopy of her body steps a baby moose, blinking at us through a thicket of brush.

"Ohmygod."

"Did you see that?"

"No bigger than a coyote."

I know this is going to be a memory because long after we've floated past them we have to force ourselves to wind forward to the next moment, the way you'd wind an old box camera to the next shot.

"Good eye," Richard says, half a kilometre later.

He admires the oddest qualities in me. I could knock myself out cooking a gourmet meal and he'd be grateful. But when I use up leftovers in the fridge, he beams across the table. If I spot a partridge, he claps me on the shoulder.

We drift by Luc's fishing party wading in the Irving pool. I can feel the subtle shift of the sun waning, the way a plane weakens on descent. One of the sports has a salmon on. Luc holds a big net and coaches him to land the fish. The other guide aims a video camera, and keeps up a steady stream of commentary.

"Starting to poop out a bit, is he?"

Just as the sport thinks he's about to pull the fish in, it takes off again, stripping line.

"Seen your pucker, he did," the man holding the camera says.

The line keeps singing.

"Big fish," Richard says in a low voice. "It's taking his line right down to the backing."

Holy Jesus. Holy Moley. Holy crap. He's got a whale on.

Their voices follow us downriver.

65

We scan the trees for a campsite, spot a clearing in the black spruce, open as the gap in a child's smile. Setting up camp takes on a kind of fervent significance.

"Leave it to me, Fire-killer," Richard says, gathering wood.

I pitch the tent, snapping the folded poles to attention and wrestling them through the slots. We don't say a word to each other, and the silence stretches out, roomy and cool as the bed when Richard goes away for the night.

If I hadn't had the provocative dream about Nathan, maybe the flirtation wouldn't have happened. He was hawk-faced and arrogant, never bragging outright about his advertising sales records, he still managed to convey his superiority in the crisp snippets of his dialogue, in the way his eyes swept over me and never lingered.

When I told Nathan about the dream over morning coffee in the staff-room, he blushed. The act of moving blood through his veins, of turning his neck splotchy, made him suddenly appealing. I imagined him building model airplanes as a boy, the fierce concentration, the oily rim of his ball cap.

We set our computers up so we could chat back and forth on line, sitting with our backs to each other in the office. Five feet of charged space between us.

In the morning, I stay wrapped in my sleeping-bag and stare at old bloodstains on the tent where I've squished mosquitoes on past trips.

"Coffee," Richard says.

My boots are covered in frost. I shove my feet in and grimace. The cold radiates to my bladder and I creep off into the bushes, turn my arms into a human toilet seat, tucking my wrists under my knees and leaning back on my haunches. I remember my shoelaces are untied and look down, but it's too late, they steam on the ground between

66

my feet like hot wires.

We pull in as close to the fire as we can without risking holes in our clothes from the flying sparks.

"Looks like a nice pool," Richard says, reading the water.

I stare at the river, but it all looks the same to me.

After breakfast we gear up for fishing. I mosey over to Richard, who is tying a fly on the end of his tippet.

"What are you putting on?"

"When all else fails..." he begins.

"...try the butterfly," I say.

I finish his sentence the way I always do, like when we play crib, "Fifteen two..." "...and the rest won't do." Or when we pass a brook on the river and raise our beer cans, "Hail to the tributary..." "...That makes the river larger."

I sift through my fly box until I find a little green bug with orange bristles. I tie it on with a clinch knot, passing the end of the tippet through the hook eye, and winding the tag end five times around itself, mouthing the numbers. Bringing the tag end back through the loop, I pull gently. It slides like a noose snug against the hook eye. If I pull too quickly it will come apart in my hands. That's the last thing I want. The line has a memory for bad knots. The secret is to know when to pull gently and when to test the line with a good tug.

I tuck my coffee cup into the chest pocket of my waders. The heat makes its way slowly through the nylon, to my solar plexus. It doesn't help. The icy water sucks at my crotch, makes my fingers numb when I pull the line in.

"Did you see that one roll?" Richard says, lobbing encouragement over his right shoulder.

I lift the line off the water and it swings over my head. The trick to casting is to take the pause at the top. Easier said than done. The natural tendency is to whip the rod back down, to give in to the false certainty that the line will collapse. I've lost a lot of flies off the tippet of my leader cracking the rod like a whip, rather than trust one second of stillness at the top of my cast.

Richard looks back and makes a zinging sound and pulls his rod up, pretending he has a monster fish on. He grins.

"I can feel it now," he says.

I smile back and nod, even though I don't go wild when a salmon smashes into my line, the way Richard does. I'm not even that interested in playing the fish. I certainly don't want to land it. The first time I hooked a salmon he refused to kill it.

"It's your fish," he said.

It took the weight of my body to pin it to the shore. No matter how many times I clubbed it on the head with the rock, the salmon kept twitching. The next time I caught a salmon, I let it go. When I lowered the fish back into the water it lay in my hands for a full minute, letting the river remember the route of its body, weighing nothing, or so I thought, until it thrashed off my fingers and was gone.

We hear Angel Falls approaching long before we see it. At first, I think the wind is playing my ears again, covering them like the skin of a drum, so that the back-up gusts have something to beat against. I turn my head sideways to break the wind barrier, but the sound remains. The air turns misty and cool.

For once, Richard exercises caution.

"If it wasn't for those two rocks at the bottom, we could run it," he says. "But if we hit either one, we'll flip for sure."

I hike down to the bottom of the falls and stand on an outcrop of rocks and watch him tie a rope to the bow of the canoe. He walks it toward the falls as if it is a wild horse he must keep his distance from. As he wades in closer to shore, he stops and fumbles with a knot in the rope. The canoe strains on the edge of the falls. Too slowly the words travel from my eyes to my brain to my mouth—*Watch out.* The canoe plunges over the falls. Holding onto the rope, Richard dives after the canoe. He has chest waders on and no lifejacket. I see his head pop up and hear him pull air into his lungs before going under again. Using the rope, he climbs hand-over-hand toward the canoe until his face is just above water. The second drop-off is much steeper. He looks at me right before he goes over.

Richard participated politely in our relationship after I told him about the flirting, as if the marriage was a machine and I was the broken part. He flat out refused to go to marriage counselling, insisting that we could find the answers in self-help books, which I bought and he never read.

At night, I soaked in porcelain anger, and began to imagine my own solutions to the problem. There was the hunting fantasy; an unfortunate accident involving Richard and one of his hunting buddies—Forest Drunk, who shot a potato gun six inches away from Richard's ear once and left it ringing for months. In the end, I feel too guilty and settle on a terminal lung disease, one that leaves him breathing on a ventilator, but too incapacitated to handle his own financial and legal affairs.

Lately, the fantasy has progressed. I finally perform an act of mercy and pull the plug.

He looks at me right before he goes over the worst section of waterfall. We almost shrug at each other, as if the future is a nagging child and we are both too tired to say no. He grabs the baseball hat off his head, tossing it toward the canoe as it plunges over. It misses and gets swept away in the froth.

Everything I know is stretched in front of me: my childhood, the arbor knot that secures my backing to the reel, and next, the fly line—momentum of every day, oh the white weight of it—and then the blood knot fixing the fly line to the leader, which is strong and clear and tapers off to the tippet, and finally the clinch knot, married to the moment, that flits and glints and presents itself, perfectly.

It's almost a relief when he goes over. I race farther downriver, to the place I imagine he is heading toward and just as I am about to dive into the water, Richard resurfaces at the bottom of the rapids. He has managed to free himself of his waders. Following the rope up with his hands, he grabs the stern of the canoe in the crook of his arm and wrestles it to the opposite shore like a crocodile. We stand looking at each other, the river caught between us. Whatever we shout at each other now is lost in the roar of rock and water.

Rarely Blue

Jennifer inhales smoke from her chocolate-flavoured cigar and relishes the hard stares of jealous women whose boyfriends sniff the air around her with approval. She puffs harder, faster. The final game of the Stanley Cup is playing out on the giant sports screen and although the sound is low, Jennifer can hear the cheering hockey fans as they make an occasional breakaway through the dance floor thump.

Johnny Cole's face fills the screen, bordered in red and mounted above impressive statistics. More hockey card than human. She has a card something like it at home that she got at the flea market, that she swapped a twelve-year-old card hustler for, in return for her Johnny Cole story: a plumped up tale of Grade-10 romance, ending with the worse trade in hockey history, the dumping of the future hockey star by Jennifer, in exchange for Greenbank High defenceman, Nigel Nickerson, knocked out of the sport with a knee injury before his seventeenth birthday.

In fact, there are two Johnny Cole stories. The second of which is not up for trade. Although she hints at it, stinger-style. *We hooked up again when I was twenty. But that's another story.*

Always leave them wanting more.

Jennifer is twenty, and nibbling the centre of the toast, leaving a pile of crust on her plate in a vain attempt to lure her father into one of his bread debates. *Everybody knows the crust's the best part of the loaf.* He ignores her effort. In between sloppy spoonfuls of Shreddies he continues to ring off the final NHL scoring statistics for the season. John Cole has finished up in third place.

"Whoop-dee-doo," Jennifer says, brushing crumbs into the sink.

"He's probably dating Brooke Shields right now," her father says.

He strokes a yellow highlighter through Johnny's scores.

Jennifer may well have remained indifferent to her ex-boyfriend's fame, if her father had not clipped every article written about him out of the newspaper over the past few years and taped them to the refrigerator door. Her dad says Johnny Cole is right up there with Gretzky and Messier. He should know. He follows John's hockey as if it is his own son's career.

Every time her dad boasts about her having dated a hockey star, Jennifer wants to jump in and scream, *It was for one month in Grade 10 for God's sake*! But she never does.

When her dad leaves for work, Jennifer can't resist flipping through the sport section. There he is, in a photo from his last game, the body leaning at an impossible angle, ice shooting from his skates like sparks. His heart does not thump. It thwacks. She squints at his blurry face in the picture. His nose had changed. It looks well acquainted with the ends of sticks and fists and elbows.

Jennifer pushes the screen door open and steps outside. Movers grunt up and down the driveway across the street, shouldering carpet. Every row house on her street is painted green. The same colour worn by the last army base she lived on. Moving trucks jut out on both sides of the street like teeth in a zipper.

"Go look for a job," her mother yells, from somewhere deep inside the house.

Jennifer sits on the front step in the weak sun.

"I have one."

She counts to five. Her mother reaches the door, huffing behind her.

"Working the Canex four hours every Saturday won't pay for school."

Jennifer stands up and brushes the dirt off the bottom of her shorts. She can hear her mother's voice wafting through the screen when she reaches the end of the driveway.

"You're not sitting around this house all summer."

What does she care if goes to back to school in the fall? She'll have to spend another year upgrading. Her marks are still too low for the computer program her father has offered to pay for. Whenever she mentions Art College he throws another statistic out. *Ninety percent of people hate what they're doing.*

Jennifer strolls by the two movers who are now wrestling the Williams' dresser through the front door. From the corner of her eye she can see one of them signal the other. They stop struggling until she's well passed.

Later that night, Jennifer's mother comes into her bedroom, clutching the newspaper in a red soapy hand. Johnny Cole is coming to Halifax on the weekend to sign autographs in support of Kids At Risk.

"This is a chance to shut your father up once and for all," she says.

For the rest of the week, Jennifer's dad pretends that he has no interest in the whole affair. But he gets all the details through her mother who then carries his suggestions carefully back to Jennifer.

"We'll just happen to be walking through the mall," her mother says.

Friday night. Jennifer tugs on a pair of jeans and a yellow tank top. She looks tanned and fit. Her mom pops her head in the bathroom just as she is applying a tissue to her second coat of lipstick.

"Nice colour."

Jennifer reads the bottom of the lipstick tube.

"Captive," she says.

Her father drives them to the shopping centre and drops them off at the front doors.

"You got one hour."

They watch the car pull away. *He thinks you should tuck your shirt in*, her mother says. Although Jennifer's dad did

73

not utter one word during the ride to the mall, she has no doubt that what her mother says is true. It is the osmotic nature of their relationship, hers too, for that matter. Except she leaves the shirt out.

They loop through the shopping centre, past the lure of T-shirt racks and shoe bins. Malls makes Jennifer feel tired the way hospitals make her feel ill. They are almost past the drugstore before she notices the booth. Even though she has come to see John, she is shocked at the sight of him, bent over signing a hockey card.

He straightens up and looks right at her.

She forgets about the speech she has rehearsed with her mother. She forgets about the shocked expression.

"Remember me?"

"Yes, I do."

"It's Jennifer," she says, not wanting to risk his forgetting her name.

She back-paddles into her routine; how she is out shopping for a birthday present with her mother, how she saw him standing here, and what a shock, and what on *earth* are you doing in Halifax? They chat for almost an hour, in between countless autographs, and handshakes, and hockey stories. She stands off to one side and tries to look interested but not too impressed. John looks embarrassed by the attention. Her mother strolls past and taps her watch.

"I'm heading downtown tonight with a couple of players," John says.

When Jennifer gets home she calls up her friend Nicky to see if she wants to go bar hopping. Nicky has great clothes that she is willing to lend, and a mysterious tan 365 days of the year.

She met Nicky the year before at university. Whenever Jennifer skipped classes and hung out at the Student Union Building, Nicky was there, holding court on a sofa in the green room with the Greek guys who smoked Camel cigarettes and twirled worry beads. When a friend introduced them one day, Jennifer discovered that Nicky didn't actually attend university. She had blown every cent of her tuition money on clothes and parties.

Nicky's father dropped her off on campus every morning in his taxi, and picked her up at the end of the day. She carried her fictitious assignments around in a designer briefcase. Her father was Lebanese and didn't know anything about the Canadian school system. Nicky had convinced her parents that school marks weren't assigned until the very end of the program.

She has two years left to think of something else.

That evening, at the dinner table, Jennifer's father drops his car keys onto her lap.

"You're lending me your car?" Jennifer says. "What about insurance? I thought I wasn't covered?"

"Do you want it or not?" he asks, without waiting for an answer.

Jennifer drives to Nicky's place. The front of Nicky's house has huge marble pillars, but on the inside, every room in the house is unfinished, plywood floors are splattered with paint, wires twist from the outlets.

They spend two hours in Nicky's bedroom trying on different outfits and posing in front of the full length mirror. Nicky's mother comes in the room again and again demanding to know where they're going. No matter how many times Nicky insists they are heading to the church party, her mother isn't satisfied. When she switches from English to Arabic, Jennifer gets nervous. She has seen her slap Nicky in the face before, following a barrage of Arabic shrieking and similar hand-waving gestures.

Regardless of how worked up she gets at Nicky she is always sweet to Jennifer.

"You have face and hair of angel," she says, stroking Jennifer's blond hair.

Luckily, her efforts begin to sag before she reaches the slapping stage. She appears more haggard with every entrance, until finally she shoos them away with a slow wave of the hand.

Jennifer has settled on a blue pair of Nicky's pants, a red polo shirt, and a white jacket.

"Very nautical," Nicky says, approvingly.

They spend two hours trawling the downtown bars, weaving through bodies as if they are underwater. Jennifer nods at people she knows but doesn't stop. She presses on through the waves of music and skin.

"Can we *please* stop for a drink?" Nicky says.

On the way to the back bar in Pirate's Cove, Jennifer sees John leaning against a post, dressed in an off-white suit. When he spots her watching him, she sees something catch in his eyes. They spend the night together on the dance floor. She does not see Nicky leave.

When the lights come on at closing time, Jennifer is drunk.

They creep through the front door of Jennifer's house using their hands to eat laughter like ice cream. The light snaps on. Jennifer's mother appears in the entranceway. Her frown lifts when she sees John.

"You kids must be hungry."

"I'll have a grilled cheese," Jennifer says.

Dressed in a nightgown and slippers, she hands them napkins and serves them nachos from a tray. It is three in the morning. Her mother insists John spend the night.

"Jennifer's a little *too* tipsy to get back behind the wheel," she says, with a tight smile.

She scurries down the hall to make up the guest bed.

When Jennifer goes to the bathroom to brush her teeth, her mother slips in behind her.

"Keep your sweat pants on, stay above the covers and leave the door open."

Jennifer is shocked. She can't believe this is coming from the same woman who flicks the basement lights on and off whenever she brings a guy downstairs. Or even worse, runs

76

up and down the stairs pretending to need preservatives from the cold storage.

Jennifer's first reaction to her mother's suggestion that she share John's bed is to worry about her father's reaction. Then she puts one and one together. If she is allowed to sleep in the guest-room with John, the order must have come from up high. She salutes her mother and says goodnight.

"Don't forget to show him your scrapbook," her mother whispers.

Jennifer pulls a big red book down from her bedroom closet, filled with newspaper articles about the Miss Halifax pageant that her mother carefully clipped out. There she is—waiting to hear the judge's decision, there she is—roses being pressed into her arms, there she is—tiara perched precariously on her head.

"It must have been a great experience," John says politely. "Do you still paint?"

He convinces her to dig out some of her artwork, pausing to study one of her favourite paintings. She started it last year when they were on summer holidays. It is a picture of her mother sitting on a big rock with her shoes off. It's Jennifer's favourite because of the smile. Her dad had lost patience when she was sketching and stomped off in search of a newspaper. Without his usual coaching, "Come on Doris, smile, not like *that*," her mother had relaxed. Jennifer captured the rare moment.

"How would you even think to use blue and yellow for skin colour. Or purple and green for sky?"

"That's the way I see it, I guess."

"Skin looks beige to me," John says, "Sky looks blue."

Jennifer laughs and tells him to close his eyes.

"What does the roof of your mouth feel like?" she asks.

John is surprised by his own lengthy description.

"Your tongue doesn't feel it anymore, right? The same way people stop seeing colour. The sky is rarely blue. We think we're looking at it, but we're seeing it through memory. Sometimes I think we only ever really see something the first time we set eyes on it."

Jennifer lies down next to him. She can feel him holding back. He starts to say something but she kisses away whatever words are waiting for her.

The next morning Jennifer hears the hiss of bacon and sausages down the hall. The sound makes her queasy. When she slips her arm out from beneath John, he opens his eyes.

"What time is it?" he asks.

A vase that Jennifer has never seen before is sitting on the table filled with plastic flowers, still damp from the swipe of a rag. Her mom has laid out the table for breakfast like it is Sunday night supper. Jennifer looks expectantly for the little crystal dishes filled with mustard pickles, and chow-chow.

Her dad is at the stove, pivoting between frypans.

"How do you like your eggs, John?"

"I'll have mine poached," Jennifer says.

When breakfast is served, the whites of Jennifer's fried eggs are gooey and clear, the sausages—pink, in the centre. This is family tradition. Whenever her father suspects her of being hungover, he serves her a huge under-cooked breakfast, insisting she eat every bite. "How's that greasy pork feel sliding down your throat?" Jennifer notices that John's bacon is crispy. His eggs don't jiggle. The guys talk hockey over coffee in the living-room, while Jennifer and her mother bend silently around each other in the kitchen.

Before John leaves he jots down her phone number, promising to call after the charity luncheon. He is in town for one more night. Jennifer's dad offers to drive him back to his hotel.

Stepping out the front door, Jennifer notices with horror that she has missed most of the driveway and parked on the front lawn. She waves goodbye as the car pulls away. Her father does not wave back.

Inside the house, her mother is waiting.

"Well? Well?" she chants.

"He's engaged," Jennifer says, heading back to bed.

Five years later, Jennifer strains to catch the tinny voice of the broadcaster's play-by-play beneath the deep insistency of bass. There are two minutes remaining in the game. John's team hasn't won the Stanley cup in over 30 years. The score is tied.

He did not call Jennifer before leaving Halifax. Even knowing that he wouldn't call, she had hung around the house until she was absolutely certain he had left town. Her father did not mention the drinking and driving, or the sleepover. In fact, he never mentioned Johnny Cole again. The front of the refrigerator remained bare except for the picture of Jesus, crucified by a green and white golfball magnet, coloured in with a pen years before when Jennifer was tiptoe-tall enough to slide them down.

JASPREET SINGH

Spellbound

A menstrous woman's touch blasts the fruits of the field, sours wine, clouds mirrors, rusts iron, and blunts the edges of knives —Pliny.

The scientist was so good-looking we all found it impossible to work in the lab. Therefore, we started working in the evenings and over weekends. Many times we had to skip Sunday church. We stopped entertaining kids and spouses and business clients. We sacrificed Super Bowl games. There was no other option.

We were almost offended by his beauty. He could bring the entire lab to a halt with his hazy lamellar smile. His beauty mesmerized us in the middle of our bench tests and mathematics. His gazelle-eyes left us spellbound. The force field automatically oriented us in his direction no matter what corner we occupied, no matter how deeply involved we were in projects. Those of us in different rooms were compelled to use the peepholes in the door, or look in the reflecting mirrors, or on the turbid glass flasks. To be out of sight from his beauty produced a strange diabolic guilt. His body was the effort of a nineteenth century artist-alchemist that pulls one toward the vanishing point—the point without co-ordinates. At times his eyes lit up with sublime reddish-blue fire. The glare was stronger than that of welding torches but we could stare for hours without hurting our retinas.

We, the male research technicians (also known as T2s) in the absorbency lab, took the scientist's beauty seriously. We cross-sectioned the moist emissions from his eyelids, quenched them with liquid nitrogen slush, freeze-dried the samples and conducted a battery of analysis. At first we failed to detect even small traces of beauty; we saw nothing more than tones of yellow sepia. However, when we used non-linear calibrations the CAT scans confirmed our conjectures, spectroscopes produced peaks of unblemished beauty, X-ray images validated the dazzling phenomenon.

The managers denied the data at first. They denied despite rigorous reports from clinical T2s. They refused to buy PET scanners and automated mannequins to discover the heart of beauty. We were not surprised, just frustrated. Our managers spoke like used-car salesmen, they always yelled at brilliant ideas.

No research for research's sake.

This is how the mind works, the mind of the most myopic and useless creatures in the world.

The managers suspected infiltration, that he had come from the competitor's lab to cast a cheap spell on us and steal the secrets of absorbency. But the secretary with the sickly face said that he belonged to our own corporation. Didn't you notice, she said, he speaks with a strong accent, his "p" sounds like "b," his "t" sounds like "d," his "v" and "w" are identical.

K.B!

K.B. was a foreigner. Foreigners give rise to curiosity, envy, fear. Rarely do they evoke beauty or seduce with a sea of beauty. Foreigners should not draw attention to themselves, at least not more than they deserve. Foreigners mimic, they don't conjure up a new reality.

K.B. had no visible signs of beauty when the managers hired him. He was an ordinary expert in absorbency. He was hired to model the flow of baby urine and to climb the corporate totem pole. He was not there to electrify people's blood. The secretary with the sickly face thought baby urine beautified K.B. Absolutely wrong. The step change happened when he began work on tampons and menses. Menses gave his face the damask sheen. Menses made him beautiful.

Menses is no ordinary fluid like water or baby urine. It is a complex fluid, a paste of big but gentle molecules—which mutate as they flow. Sadly, there isn't enough menses in the world to do tampon testing. A menstrous woman produces barely 30 ml of menses per month. Sadly, no two samples of menses donated by women are identical. In fact, there is no such thing as menses; what we have are tens of thousands different kinds of fluids, all categorized under "menses" for want of a better word. The sample-to-sample variation is so huge an entire elephant can pass through the data points. Worst: the production of menses obeys the laws of Chaos. A small change in initial conditions like memories, dreams, desires, drugs and moods, etc, can cause a large change in the final consistency of a gush of menses.

K.B. rescued our company. He arrived at the tampon lab at a critical time and said yes to the challenge. He was a pure scientist, with a vision to help the women of the world to uncover the secrets of absorbency. He developed a simulant, a fluid substitute that mimicked menses. K.B. invented a fluid more real than real menses.

We, the T2s, were assigned by the managers to work with K.B. Our job was purely mechanical, so we saw the research star in action. Watching him, we lost our fear and disgust and jokes about menses. Before K.B. no-one in the lab was particularly fond of complex fluids. We were repelled by videos of absorbents wicking menses from vaginas. Streams of leaked menses horrified us; they always vanished somewhere in the pubic hair. Menses odour control tests made us throw up, vomit. Before K.B. we felt fluids like phlegm and runny-BM were more civilized than menses.

K.B. energized the menses lab. Right from day one we were on a first name basis, but when he was in professorial mode he called us "teckies." His "Teckies, plot time versus flow-rate," sounded like "Deckies, blood dime versus flow-red."

K.B. developed the first-of-a-kind menses simulant in barely nine months. He used five things: chicken-eggs, pig-blood, virgin superabsorbing-gel, moonlight, and time. He stirred the chicken-eggs and pig-blood magnetically and poured them into a barrel made of sticky and amorphous superabsorbing-gel. He used chicken eggs because they contain proteins. He preferred pig-blood because its red-blood-cell count is identical to that of a woman's blood. For details see US Patent No. Usonia–107, 308, 110 (Also, in case you are wired, check out a fine site on menses: http://www.mum.org).

The secret of menses lies in the uterine shell of the gel. A barrel made from a young or an old gel always gives bad menses. There exists an optimum age when a gel attains the precise softness, warmth and marigold odour. Ideal menses comes from natural gels, which grow in marshlands, in the darkness of the night. Such gels have basked in the moon. There is more moonlight in them than there is chlorophyll in the leaves.

On moonlit nights, the nights when the simulant matured, K.B. poured a vial of real menses into a barrel. He stripped out of his lab coat and descended into the barrel and tasted the contents from his cupped hands and declared: *I think it is done, teckies, plus or minus 5%.*

Inside the barrel, menses went to his head as if by osmosis.

The fluid devoured his flesh and bone, and coagulated him into a blob of beauty. He arose from the depths with an incandescent smile, spilling claret fluid and purple shadows. Sometimes he bit his lips and wiped colloids off his eyelids and spoke softly: *Menses is not just another fluid, teckies, it is the complex history of life itself, the smell of our birthblood, the jelly of our death. Period.* His long hair, plastered to his neck and shoulders, sparkled with red dewy brilliance. The particles caught in the hair looked like caviar and left us breathless.

K.B.'s beauty burned the managers and their deputies into charcoals. They reported him to Upper Management. "People work," said the Director, "only for rewards or to save their butts. K.B.'s case is different. He works because he is passionate...honestly, he is beautiful because he works beautifully...wants to know the truth; his work is pure because he is in permanent exile from his homeland...none of us here could become beautiful like him...let's all go to Patagonia or forget it."

Upper Management soon recognized the only two options before the company: (1) to engineer beauty out of existence or (2) to adapt to it. They chose to patent Beauty. They brought in lawyers and filed patent applications at the U.S. Patent Office. They claimed a brand-new invention—novel and non-obvious. After two appeals the patent was granted.

US PATENT NO. USONIA–112, 358, 420:
HIGH BEAUTY CONTENT FOREIGN MALE AND A METHOD FOR MAKING IT.

ABSTRACT:

The present invention is directed to a human male who contains high concentrations of foreign accent and who exhibits high levels

of beauty. The invention is further directed to methods for manu-
facturing such beauty from menses and/or menses simulant.

CLAIMS:

What is claimed is:
1. *High level of beauty*
2. *The beauty of Claim 1, wherein the said beauty comprises visibility.*
3. *The beauty of Claim 2, wherein the said beauty comprises exactitude.*
4. *The beauty of Claim 3, wherein the said beauty comprises lightness.*
5. *The beauty of Claim 4, wherein the said beauty comprises quickness.*
6. *The beauty of Claim 5, wherein the said beauty comprises multiplicity.*
7. *The beauty of Claim 6, wherein the said beauty comprises consistency.*
8. *Method for manufacturing the said beauty.*
9. *The method according to Claim 8, wherein the said method comprises chicken eggs.*
10. *The method according to Claim 9, wherein the said method comprises pig-blood*
11. *The method according to Claim 10, wherein the said method comprises virgin superabsorbing gel.*
12. *The method according to Claim 11, wherein the said method comprises moonlight.*
13. *The method according to Claim 12, wherein the said method comprises time.*

Although the patent was granted, no-one in the lab understood the mechanism or the inevitable consequences of
beauty. Models and metaphors failed us. Handbooks of
Bio-chemistry and Physics and Mathematics provided no
answers. Our outside contracts, professors in Ivy League

universities, whose opinion we valued, scratched their heads. The riddle of beauty had no solution. Poets, the champions of the irrational, were of no help. Beauty is not caused, it is (Emily Dickinson).

K.B. didn't understand his own mutation well. He had no idea why his beauty crowded our lives. We were witnessing the throes of a brand-new force, much like the force of gravity, and didn't know the full potential of the force, or its appropriate name. Frustrated with the pseudo-science of patents, the research fellows in our lab wrote a technical letter to *Nature*. The letter appeared next to the editorial section. Our esteemed management fumed as a result. The managers considered Beauty an intellectual property issue, they desired confidentiality. *Nature*'s broad readership didn't show much enthusiasm. Skeptics and mediocre scientists ridiculed the discovery of "beauty," and labelled our work as "ironic." They tried to demolish our method to plot beauty, our use of the logarithmic scale.

Meanwhile K.B.'s beauty crossed all prescribed boundaries, it grew a trillion times. We almost lost the ability to do science. The moment he put on his lab coat—moon-dew formed around his liquid eyes. By the time he slipped his hands into the vinyl gloves a dense cloud of dew started spiralling toward us. The moment he began experiments on the flow of complex-fluids the cloud struck us like soft metallic rain. His beauty made us remove our engagement and wedding rings; we thought about him more than our lovers; we spilled our deepest secrets before him. He made us throb like the dark veins of a delirious mist. Our dreams acquired the taste of pomegranates.

However, the process engineers pointed to the precipitous drop in line efficiency—the tampon lines plummeted from 2000 tampons per minute to 20 tampons per minute. The women of the world started losing faith in our company. Business magazines wrote us off. The chairman of the safety board alarmed us about the hazards of exposure to Beauty. Our marriages started falling apart; the Church complained about the rising divorce rate. The marketing men ruthlessly widened the gap between K.B., the scientist, and the new tampon brand they had launched. The brand was a variant of talc-impregnated-mensesphilic-polyurethane foam with resilient-ellipsoid fibres and K.B.'s face and fragrance on the outer cover.

The Upper management felt threatened by the fiend who had contaminated our lives. K.B. started mixing science with religion. "He is breaking up," the Director wrote in the performance review. He was right, but he had no idea about the pattern—all great scientists say anomalous things. K.B.'s sermons on death and dying made absolutely no sense. One day he stepped out of the menses barrel and declared: *Teckies, I have figured the two key axioms of beauty. Beauty crowds us till we die. The day we die God holds her hands on her belly and She menstruates.*

The CEO and Chairman of the Board fired K.B. on Memorial Day. It was a painful decision. But it was also a rational decision. They based it on the joint recommendation of Process, Safety, Marketing and the *Wall Street Journal.* Official reason: *He did research for research's sake.* Unofficial reason: Profit per share dropped by nineteen cents.

The Vice President of Research personally ordered masked men to bleach beauty out of the lab and away from the tampon plants. The masked men dumped millions of gallons of beauty-active waste in the lakes. Despite their best efforts, it was obvious, we had been contaminated for life.

K.B. was escorted out of the lab by two neolithic security guards. Most of us snarled and squealed and sniggered as the tableau passed by. We did this to keep our jobs; the managers were watching. In the lobby, K.B. stopped before the big mirror. He tiptoed to see his entire face in the mirror. The neolithic men tore the sleeve of his lab-coat. K.B. looked traumatized, his eyes burnt with anger and sadness, but his beauty remained undiminished. Watching him in that torn lab-coat we realized he was a breathing human being like the rest of us. His beauty must have condemned him to solitude, more than the pedestrian solitude of a permanent exile. While he stood in front of his serene image we were forced to examine our own sterile lives, petty ambitions and ugliness. Our lives paled before the stains and markings on his lab-coat. Yet we howled and yelled and sniggered.

He winked and turned and walked away in innocence and pride and beauty.

We picked up the torn sleeve spontaneously and wrapped a mylar film around it and froze it in liquid helium. Then we cross-sectioned a sample and looked at it under a cryo-SEM. The markings on the sleeve were all dumb-bell shapes of red colour; however, some continued to grow redder and redder, which is normal for bloodstains formed under traumatic conditions.

Two days after K.B. was expelled from the corporate gates, the absorbency lab was struck by a moon-drizzle, which was wicked away, at that very instant, by the grey walls of the whole building. We saw a silver wave speeding toward the beauty-bleached tampons, dazzling prematurely in ten, 50, 100,000 cardboard boxes. The silver wave broke finally into an intense glow. Darkness followed, which was inevitable. The whole world forgot Beauty, which was also inevitable.

However, the women in the supermarket aisles in 137 countries came to know, all of a sudden, the secret of absorbency, because although Beauty didn't exist anymore, its glance and gesture had dissolved into their very blood.

A Little Bit of Bar-rough

Beware of what comes out of Montreal, especially during winter. It is the force corrosive to all human institutions—Leonard Cohen.

Greek symbols flicker on your Jackie-O dress. Blue light from the projector lights the freckles on your face. You stand cross-ankled between the screen and the source of light.

Your presentation is concise, passionate, shall I say funky.... The audience is mesmerized by your nyloned legs and precise fingers—bluish elongated fingers. You turn your back toward us, mostly chemistry men with hairy knuckles. You rise on your toes, point at images; place a hand behind, on the hem of your short dress.

"This is *Ice-7*," you say. "*Ice-7* melts at 100°C. *Ice-1* is ice-cube ice. *Ice-8* sinks in water."

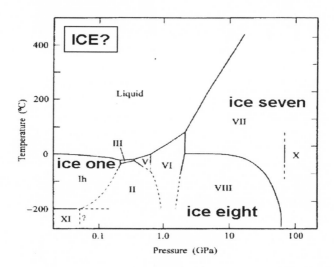

I would like to sink in water, chérie. Your waters run deep, chérie. My lips are still kindled with kisses you planted in the taxi on the way back from the airport. I have drifted far from this conference-room, where you continue inflecting words in that characteristic French manner, I mean the Canadian French manner. I'm like a rich man entering heaven through the waves and particles of your sounds. You add "h" to "eight," drop "h" from "height." It is "ard" to cover "heverything."

After explaining the so-called pressure-temperature graphs of ice, you show us the pictures.

"Ice is the Mona Lisa of science," you say. "These high-resolution pictures were taken using an atomic microscope. Our microscope 'touched' ice samples to 'see' all the hidden things. This technique is called—*Seeing by Touching*.

"The delicate tip (of our microscope's cantilever) touched the samples in two ways: (a) Contact way, (b) Tapping way. Let me give you an analogy, ladies and gentlemen: Please, each one of you, move a finger on the back of your hand. Do not lift the finger as you move it from one side to another. Oui, oui, exactly the way you are doing it. This is the *contact way*. And now, move the same finger again, yes. But this time keep tapping the finger as it moves from one side to another. You see! Herein lies the secret of seeing-by-touching: *Tapping is better than contact. Tapping doesn't harm the specimen.*"

Applause!

Everything you say is beautiful, chérie. You and I have a *tapping* relationship, chérie. The hairy chemists in this audience reek of the secret police employed by your husband.

You *pro mice* the audience hard copies of your images.

"Is it *pro-miss* or *pro-mice?*" you beg me to clarify after the presentation. There is linguistic embarrassment in your laughter.

"Pro-miss-ing or pro-mice-ing?"

"I too have problems with English," I say.

This, our third rendezvous, has begun without problems. Again, I've risked the dangerous visit, my third trip from India to attend the conference on pollution in Montreal. Your city. Embalmed city. Mont-unreal.

Bar-rough. In my language both snow and ice are known by the same word.

After the presentation you install me at the Ritz; stay over. You wash your peroxide hair with micellar herbs, sing Leonard Cohen and Emile Nelligan for hours strumming that handsome unvarnished guitar.

I mimic material from the presentation: *Tapping is better than contact because it doesn't harm.*

"Forget...microscopic...jargon," you say. "Chéri, forget... it." You have this annoying but adorable habit to pause, search for the precise word. (You seduced me with this habit. I grasped the little rocks of your habit).

Still in my un-Canadian clothes I repeat your favourite words—the "hill-stations" and "monsoons" and "colonial lunatic asylums."

"Chéri," you say, "colonial hasylums...in ill-stations... haway...from monsoons...oui, that is where we should elope to."

94

Nadia, my wife in India, if she finds out, will banish me from her heart, forever.

I swish open the curtains. Outside, on the street, the weight of snow has twisted the bikes. The young woman waiting at the bus-stop looks like a comical Bedouin. Dunes have formed on her cheekbones, humps on her ears. Mad Montreal is hurting her into a poem—

Ah! Comme la neige a neigé !
Ma vitre est un jardin de givre.
Ah! comme la neige a neigé !
Qu'est-ce que le spasme de vivre
À la douleur que j'ai, que j'ai !

You are in that buoyant outdoorsy mood again. Sitting on the edge of the neatly made bed, you have put your boots on. I tie your laces, follow you to the snow-entombed rue St. Laurent. I feel like dying in your arms—tes bras tenders et doux.

Vitreous snow bites my Indian blood mercilessly on la rue; what keeps me going are the A LOVER signs outside shops and houses.
    "Non, non," you say. "À LOUER means TO LET, FOR RENT."

I notice a trail of fresh looking tracks.

Your face has turned strawberry-red, tomato-red. The wobbly cross on the mountain shivers in white powder, huge ghostly halos around it. Flakes funnel down dancing, settling on green roofs. Green, the colour of rusted copper. Green, the colour of god. Green on cathedral tops—dying a temporary death because of the flakes. You embrace me— me in the borrowed hide jacket. You wipe snow off my glasses—your bluish elongated fingers leave behind oily smears and funky fragrance.

Nadia, my love, if she finds out, will exile me from her heart, forever.

"Chéri why do you stoop while walking?—we are not walking in monsoon...rain."

Your complaint raises my chest; I reclaim swagger. I reclaim your face. The space above your eyebrows is an arch of god's powder.

Glued to you, kissing you, I stumble. Shrieking winds shove our feet slowly into a pool of slush, chubby mocha slush.... *Canadian winter is a bitch.* But you resuscitate me, you kiss ten trillion muddy flakes off my face. A film of hydrogen bonds forms between the parched skin of our lips and freezes into ice—*ice-9*. Only in Mont-unreal I realize I possess lips. You know I come from an un-kissing culture.

Yesterday, hours before the Pollution Conference, my transatlantic airbus landed on a carpet of hexagons of snow. The immigration guards were burly like their species all over the world, like the guards of my own country. Every time I return, they chew my passport as if it listed the deeds of a bio-terrorist.

In the lounge you were waiting for me muffled in mild blue knits. Your smile was soft and pure and smelled of all good things of snow.

"Minou," you asked, "this time...wat hexcuse...did you give your unsuspecting wife?"

"No hexcuse," I said. "She knows the locations of all my conferences."

"Oui-oui...."

"And you?"

You called your hubby from the airport. Outside *bar-rough* was falling softly, softly freefalling.

You handed the receiver to me. Your hubby didn't suspect a thing. "Move over to our Victorian house," he said. "We can accommodate thirteen people in our thirteen rooms."

"Mr. Queneau," I said politely, "there is a decent hotel next to the conference site."

I fear Mr. Queneau. One day he will stab us during the moment of passion.

"You globe-trotting chemists!" he chuckled. "Okay, tell me, Monsieur Chemist, which one is a better diaper—Huggies or Pampers?"

You have a two-year-old and a three-month-old and a blond Labrador. I have no problems with them. The problem is *your hubby*. He always wants to show me down. How many times do I have to remind him that I am not a diaper man?

"Mr. Q," I said nervously, "I'm a *solid-state* chemist from India...diapers are not my expertise.... But, your wife's presentation begins shortly.... On our way we are. By the way in India we call diapers *nappies*."

Good, the buffoon didn't attend your presentation. Otherwise, chérie, you might not have stayed over.

Day 2. Your talk is over. Mine too. Fine thing for our blossoming careers.

We skip *other* presentations and panels and super-panels. We follow the narrow track to the lake on the mountain. Lac Castor—the paralyzed eye of Montreal. Your dog ambles along.

Deceptive sun swims through crystal blue skies before colliding with the dog. The dog is not surprised. The lake is frozen. The dog is not surprised. This dog is not surprised by anything. Not by the bluish-green slab underneath the frozen lake. "This lake, chérie, is the diagram of our slippery romance." Now, he is surprised.

Monsieur Labrador, cold-confused, blind in one eye, goes round and round in circles. He dances like a deranged atomic-tip—which makes me arch my brows and laugh a belly laugh, but deep inside I am afraid of breaking bones on the lubricious lake.

You glide on the lake like some coral island creature. You belong to the calcite constellation of anemones and polyps. Even your Lab knows how to perform Nureyev ballets on slippery surfaces...but he has the animal advantage over me, two front legs and two hind.

If your husband had accompanied us he might have asked curious questions about diapers for dogs.

"Chéri...let's skip stones on the lake."
    "But, but, the lake is like a lens of ice."
    "Just do it."
    "I'm not your dog."

"Good dog," you jump. With gritty snow-crusted paws Monsieur Lab prowls back to you—carrying in his mouth the stick you threw toward the middle of the lake. Huffing and puffing, the one-eyed leopard discharges bellows of white smoke in the air.

You are truly, madly, deeply displeased by my comment regarding the dog. "What do you mean—you are not my dog?"

I fall on my knees behind you; put my hands in your pockets. We admire the benzene ring on the lake, drawn by the Lab. You love the Lab more than your hubby and me—the two-day-a-year guy from the colonial hasylum.

"Good dog!"

"Take a picture, take one," I implore. You forbid using the camera and elevate the conversation from lowly dogs to the galleries of les beaux arts.
"Let's visit the Heart Museum," you suggest.
"Solid State Chemists must never visit the Art Museum."

"Move to Canada," you plead.
I am surprised. I don't want to say *distance keeps us going* or that sort of thing.
"Move to India," I mimic.
I know you would never leave the ballet-dancer behind. I walk to the other edge of the lake. "Yes, I am your dog," I

say it loud like a prepubescent boy.

"Wrrf.... Wurrf."

Lab licks my pants. You laugh a belly laughter that has little razor teeth in it.

"Yes," I say, "I am your slobbering fool."

Lab drags us further to the cemetery on the art-déco side of the mountain. You are intrigued by the Henry Moorish gravestones and the Celtic crosses and I mutter material on cremations and shamshan-ghats.

"Chéri...why this sad...face?" you are curious.

My mind has drifted away from the cemetery and the chandelier whispers of ice toward my wife Nadia in India. She has perhaps just stepped out of our house and is in the bougainvillea garden ambling on orange sand. Look, she has picked up two little frogs from the sand and has permitted them to hop on her arm. Dark monsoon clouds are building at a distance. It has happened again—the first drop of monsoon just landed on her arms. Nadia is wet, her voice moist, pearl-grey....

"Why is it I like Nadia better during these trips to Canada?"

"Chéri, come, come we have a cure...for omesickness...let's climb the mountain hall the way."

Contact is worse than tapping, chérie, because it harms.

Night 2.

No, he doesn't stab me.

He is standing by the cross on the mountain...your husband.

He is reciting Neruda holding a candle in his hand. He looks as if his tooth hurts.

"What are you two doing here?" He is curious.

You and I are still standing together, no longer touching. That man's curiosity has reduced me to a combo of warm ice, cold ashes. You are not much help. You avert your eyes.

"Look at the work of Time," he says, pointing a finger at the candle.

Time responds by dispatching a gust of wind toward him. Time flaps your hubby's cap and rustles the pages of the book in thinsulate hands; the candle drips on the poems and solidifies, quickly covering the verses, which allows the dubious poet to "improvise" the odes to artichokes, tomatoes, poutines, onions, dictionaries, separations, cities.... Time reminds: There is no need to write an ode to this insane city because it reveals all its rhymes and rhythms from the lookout point on the mountain.

He makes me recite his own verses. I have this bad habit of gladly suffering unpublished poets. Unscientific people, who don't know two things about combustion, and next to nothing about handling flames on mountains. Mont-unreal.

He wants you to recite your favourite Queneau, but you say you are in the mood for a Neruda. You don't know Spanish, yet you recite *twenty love poems* and *a song of sorrow*. Faithful French translation? You flip the pages all the way back to the table of contents and stop at the ode to salt.

A freefalling flake lands on the corner of his eye, a tear drops on the ruffling pages. You draw the structure of NaCl on the margin. He sobs, the unlucky poet, and steals my line: "*Mon amour,* one needs ten thousand atomic microscopes or a single Neruda to write an ode to your Jackie-O dresses." Good, he doesn't mention the diapers. The two-year-old is observing the northern lights from Dad's shoulders. He pulls Mr. Q's brown beard and scratches Dad's neck with a fluorescent plastic chipmunk. The three-month-old shuffles his feet and claps and cries in the pouch on Dad's back. Strong back, Mr. Q. The boys will become brilliant chemists.

This is the beginning, or shall I say the re-beginning, of my sorrows. You decide not to return to my room. "I have to go," you whisper. I hold my ground. We wave adieus at the mountain top. You step in the Lexus—back to the thirteen-room Victorian house along with the boys, Lab, and that poet. *Pleurez—*

Pleurez, oiseaux de février,
Au sinistre frisson des choses,
Pleurez, oiseaux de février,
Pleurez mes pleurs, pleurez mes roses,
Aux branches du génévrier.

This has become a pattern. For the third time it has happened the exact same way and so symmetrically. You will not see me off at the airport. You will send me two half-hearted notes in the spirit of morse-code messages from a submarine stating that you would write a longer letter later, sealed with wax, and that letter would never arrive.

A year later when I fly again to Montreal, for the conference, you will install me at the Ritz and sing Leonard Cohen and Emile Nelligan for hours strumming that handsome unvarnished guitar. And we'll discuss colonial lunatic asylums; again I'll bitch about the winter in Canada. God promise.

Tapping is better than contact because it doesn't harm.

As my two days are over, I walk back to the land of ten-thousand thunders, back to the virtuous droplets on my wife Nadia's arms, howling bougainvillea leaves, smell of drizzle on orange sand, away from the *bar-rough* and slowly disintegrating ice-six, seven, eight, and nine on your Jackie-O dresses, ready to be submerged by primitive monogamy, goblets of rain.

You Must Be

About suffering they were never wrong, the Old Masters
—W.H. Auden.

Deepa, a young and perceptive Indian in her thirties, glided out of the Delhi-New York flight in a burgundy sari. She received thousands of glances and inquisitive looks. Two respectable looking men muttered in hushed tones: *go back home—terrorist bitch*. But, she remained unterrified. She finally stopped in the middle of the arrivals lounge of the Kennedy airport.

The man waiting on the vinyl chair beamed at her with delighted brown eyes. He had an unusually large face for a short figure; and he wore a crisp white shirt, checked tie and corporate suspenders. He waved at Deepa to get her attention, but she didn't notice him. He dashed toward her.

"You must be my wife?" he asked.

Startled, she took three steps backwards. Before the man could apologize, she spoke in a gentle but commanding voice.

"Remove sunglasses, please."

The man did exactly as he was told. She opened her purse, retrieved a photo and surveyed it seriously.

"Quite right," she said, "I am your wife."

Only a month ago, Dipin Joshi, the Non-Resident Indian, had legally married Deepa Saxena, M.A. (Music), during a short trip to India. Right after the wedding ceremony Dipin flew back to New York. Deepa's family promised to despatch the girl as soon as she obtained her US visa.

Initially Dipin was reluctant to get married in this arranged way, but finally he succumbed to the advice given by his friend, Raj, a successful attorney. "America has bent its immigration for you research-chemist types," Raj had said. "Within 30 days you'll be the proud owner of a Green Card!"

"Thanks, yaar."

"Now is the time to start family."

"Only when I fall in love. The American way."

"But," Raj had said, "you must marry before the Green Card arrives. Otherwise, the immigration-wallahs of this great country won't allow your wife in US for three years."

"You only tell me what to do then."

"Fly home ASAP," Raj had advised. "With your current visa status, which is temporary, your wife could join you within a month."

"You mean, marry a stranger?"

"Strangers find it easier to love each other."

"Do you know a stranger?"

"Of course," said Raj. "My niece desires moving to America. She is beautiful. Well educated. Musical. Fine blend of East and West. Her name is Deepa Saxena."

Days before Deepa's arrival, Dipin contemplated the most efficient way to welcome her to New York. He settled on a Broadway musical. And now after having identified her properly at the airport he was in no rush to consummate the marriage in the brand-new suburban condominium, plenty of time for all that. After the initial confusion was sorted out he whistled a Bollywood song and tried sweeping her henna coloured hair away from her face with the back of his hand. She stopped the hand in mid-gesture and requested him to take care of the baggage first. Dipin used the chrome trolley to transfer her three bags and the case containing her sitar to the silvery SUV. Two hours later he pulled out toward the sinuous lights on the jammed highway. Through the sky-roof she saw the moon.

"Forget the moon," he said. "Look at the Titans!"

"And what are Titans?"

"Giants," he said, pointing at the skyscrapers through

the SUV window. "And night is the best time to look at them."

He eased at 45th, between Broadway and Eighth Avenue.

"I have a dream," he said, "to show you the best buildings and the best musicals in the city. I want you to learn as much about the American culture as you know about the sitar. Before we go home—let's check out a musical."

"Bags *toh* are in the car," she said. "On top I am so much jet-lagged."

Dipin accelerated the car abruptly. Deepa thought she might have offended him and said softly, "Let's watch the musical."

In the lobby she once again noticed hundreds of glances and inquisitive looks. "Have they never seen a sari and a bindi before?" she asked herself. And that is why she was somewhat stunned when a police officer, standing close-by, wished her *good evening ma'am*. She was impressed by the good manners of the police-wallah.

"Cops," Dipin told her. "They are keeping an eye on the middle-eastern people."

"But not all of them are bad," she said. "Don't you see, we look middle-eastern."

"This is America," he said. "Only those who commit crimes are arrested."

Deepa stood in front of the posters and Dipin hobbled toward the box-office window.

"Ma'am," he asked the white girl behind the window, "Two for *Kiss Me Kelly!*"

"*Kiss Me Kelly* is packed," she said.

"More the better! *Kiss Me Kelly* please!"

"Where would you like to sit?"

"Middle—. Right in the middle. Middle of the packed show. This way, Miss, we will kill two birds with a single stone."

"No more middle," said the girl, raising her brows.

"Check again," he insisted and handed her the credit card.

Dipin Joshi, waiting for the tickets, turned to his wife. Her profile stood out sharply against the poster. Circles of sweat covered the backside of her burgundy blouse; he could see all that even from distance. Like a cartographer he surveyed her profile, and concluded that she resembled the Upper East Side. Dipin's entire ambition at that moment condensed into a desire to caress her warm and naked body. In an un-vulgar way he peeled her sari mentally. He anticipated her smell. He was happy that he had married the authentic woman. She was swell-looking, every inch of her. Also, she played the sitar beautifully—like a mildly exotic bird takes to the air. Certainly she had potential to become a celebrity, perhaps even surpass Ravi—whatever his name is—Shankar. And he, Dipin Joshi, Deepa Saxena's husband, would do his utmost to help her. Certainly she would face some minor obstacles embracing the American society. Slowly her accent would be erased the way his accent was already erasing into elegance. She might find the American slang tough to master, but he would like to teach it to her. The trick was to mimic Americans. The problem with most immigrants was that they refused to mimic. They mocked instead.

Deepa Joshi, standing in front of the poster, was stunned by the sheer audacity of display. The man in the poster was kissing the whirling brunette he had lifted high up in the air. She blinked and frowned before the shamelessly under-dressed chorus girls and closed her eyes. Wrapped in some inner music that seemed to emerge from the poster, she imagined the conflicts and conjugal duties that awaited her back at Dipin's condominium. The awkward conversation in the car had raised many doubts. Was it for this man she left her home in another country? So self-absorbed he was. She shuffled through the instincts that guided her a month ago to say yes to his proposal, which arrived at her mother's house along with the basket of oranges and a note from Uncle Raj, the New York attorney. She was seduced less by Dipin's face in the photo and more by the America behind him. The country she didn't even understand.

The girl behind the window had the face of someone who never watched musicals. She lingered a while, and finally handed Dipin Joshi two tickets. Then she waved at the police officers. While Dipin dropped the glossy tickets in the front pocket of his shirt, the four officers posted in the lobby dashed toward the ticket window. They exchanged quick words with the girl, whose index finger kept pointing at Deepa's husband.

"Mr. Josh," said an officer, "come with us."

"What is the charge?" protested Dipin Joshi.

"Mr. Josh," they said, "you are under arrest."

A crowd formed around the officers who grabbed Dipin Joshi from behind, brought him to his knees, handcuffed him and carried him off the floor. The chief officer bragged that his men had just prevented Mr. Joshi from blowing up the theatre. "This boy is going downtown," he said.

The noise distracted Deepa. She turned away from the show posters and advanced toward the crowd.

"I'm a research chemist," grovelled Dipin Joshi, "not a middle-easterner." "She is my wife," he struggled to free himself. "Look, there."

"Oh ya.... How many wives you got, sir?" asked officer-number-one.

"Leave him alone," said Deepa Saxena, "he is innocent."

"You too speak English?" queried officer-number-two.

Officer-number-three opened the arrested man's wallet and scrutinized the visiting card. Vice President of Nano Solutions, Inc.

"Honest mistake," he muttered.

"You may go," said officer-number-four, as he un-hand-cuffed the Vice President.

Dipin felt molten worms crawling on him.

"See," he protested, "you made a big mistake."

"You resemble the Arab gentleman we are after," said officer-number-one. "We can still...."

They left him in front of the theatre manager's office.

Dipin was *sure* they wanted to apologize. His first thought was: what impression would this make on the wife? He didn't want her to conclude that she had moved from one vile country to another. This was not everyday America.

The theatre manager informed Dipin Joshi that the show had already begun. "You are half-an-hour late." He was a stout man, in a camel-coloured jacket, and he provided the details.

"Because you insisted on sitting in the middle of a packed show, Mr. Joshay, our ticketing assistant got suspicious," he explained. "But please come again and watch *Kiss Me Kelly*...on the house." Dipin frowned his brows.

"And, Mr. Joshay," he continued, "the police officers mentioned that your wife here joined you today from India. An occasion to celebrate, isn't it? Here is a small gift from the management, sir; we booked a fine room for you in Hotel Lido. Pasta and wine included."

Dipin's first thought was to spit on the manager's compensation package and leave the theatre ASAP. But he restrained himself and turned toward his wife. She was adjusting her sari. Perhaps she would reapply the lipstick next. Despite the numbness and the immobilized limbs he was seized by the desire to lie down beside her heavenly figure on some neatly made bed. She made him forget the rage that filled his eyes. He accepted the free coupons and thanked the manager.

"They made a terrible mistake," he said to Deepa as he drove the SUV past Broadway, toward Hotel Lido. On his face she saw the resolve of a man who would continue to ignore petty humiliations in the streets of America.

"I am glad we left the theatre," she said while he parked the car.

"Nothing is ruined," he said. "I am in control. Tonight is the first night of our honeymoon."

She noticed the limp in Dipin's walk when they entered the lobby. She made an attempt to hold his hand but it hurt him and she had to let go. She carefully avoided peeping into the pain in his eyes.

The Pakistani bellboy rolled the luggage behind them in a trolley. Two Filipino linen girls halted in the corridor as a mark of courtesy and smiled infectiously at the customers as soon as the elevator ejected them on the 67th floor.

Deepa led Dipin into the room. Her smile was virginal and so was the way she walked. She had never been to bed with a man. He was sure about that. Again, he tried sweeping her hair away from her face with the back of his hand; again, she prevented it.

"I thought your hand was hurting, no?" she asked.

"No, no...it will be all right soon," he said. "Those men didn't know what they were doing.... Part of their job.... These days...."

The room was a perfect square with high windows and cherry furniture. Twin paintings, depicting Japanese *Geishas* and Ansel Adam's *Yosemite Meadows*, hung behind the neatly made bed. The green sofa—which somewhat blocked the entrance to the bathroom—was wide enough to serve as an additional bed.

As soon as the bellboy left them alone she helped him wash his face. He loosened his tie and slid into the bed on his own. He didn't remove his clothes, not even the shoes.

"Now you are safe," she said.

"Please help me forget this incident," he said as he transferred the cell phone and the car keys to the side table.

With her beside him, despite the pain, he felt *great*, genuinely *great*, after a long time. In a silent prayer he thanked his attorney-cum-friend, Raj, and the US visa regulations, which had brought them together. She had arrived in his life with a vast meadow of music, the meadow where he could forget the calamities of exile. He wondered if she felt equally *great*. He desired to say to her: *rub me all over my legs and arms with the wild flowers in the meadow*. But he restrained himself.

She opened the window. She heard sounds she had never heard before. She was swamped by noises from several storeys below, all the unforgiving noises that waft about in an alien city. She cupped her ears and looked at the skyscrapers, one at a time.

From the edge of the bed Dipin watched his wife's burgundy hips. Gentle. Graceful. Opulent.

"Over there. Look," he pointed.

"I am tired of looking," she said, without turning.

But he was insistent.

"You see the empty space between those two Titans?" he said.

"Looks like a valley."

Now that is where the World Trade Centre stood once upon a time.

"Oh my God!"

"No. No. The WTC towers were on the other side," he said. "Anyways," he muttered with naïve confidence, "this city will come out of this ever more stronger."

She uncupped her ears and closed the window and sat on the sofa, her eyes cast downwards. She slipped her feet out of the sandals and raised both legs on the sofa. She crossed her legs like a woman in a temple.

Dipin caught her reflection in the silver tray on the table in front of her. He was seized by the desire to sit on the arm of the sofa and kiss some prohibited part of her body much like the man in the poster for the musical. Her fragile waist, her ankleted ankles, the dark of her armpits.

Dipin poured Sauvignon Blanc into two glasses.

"Please lie down," she insisted. "What you need is more rest."

"Let us lie down," he mumbled.

"Did you say something?"

"Yes...the theatre manager," he said with complacent superiority, "the man looked kind of gay."

She shrugged.

"And what does a gay man look like?" she asked.

He didn't move back to the bed. He sat down with some difficulty on the carpet not far from her sofa.

"To our marriage!" he raised the glass. "I am thirsty."

Educated in a convent school in India, Deepa followed his instructions meticulously on how to hold the glass and to smell the thing before swallowing—with an appearance of familiarity.

She stretched her legs and crossed her small feet on the table. He refilled her empty glass. Slowly he placed his hand on her feet.

"No," she said and shrank back from him. "Not now."

"But...."

"Because...."

Deepa's closest friend in Delhi while packing the luggage had advised her to share her past with Dipin before the touching began. "Indian men who live in America," the friend said, "become dangerous. They divorce their wives if they don't find soap in the bathroom two days in a row.... Above all, beware of their sweet tongues—they use special technologies to make a woman spill out her darkest secrets. Best is to begin the marriage with a clean slate."

She noticed, as he withdrew to the bed, that he was not entirely handsome. Patches of baldness covered his head; his bird-like nose was sprayed with blackheads; his eyes wandered. His face was scabrous like an army-man's. She would work on him. She would eliminate most of his defects. In the area of chemistry, however, he had no defects. One day he was destined to become the President of his company, his family had told her. She, too, after this brief interaction, saw in him an ability to forget the past and focus entirely on the future. But how was she going to say *it* to him?

Several times, from his new position, Dipin raised his glass and squinted through it at her yawning figure, no, no, several figures of his wife, no, several of his wives, at least ten, shadows included. The wine had an unforgettable wiggle in it; he would remember the taste for the rest of his life. But.... Perhaps tonight wasn't the night for initiations despite love and lust spilling within him. She was resisting sleep despite jetlag locked in her temples. Taking her to the theatre wasn't a good idea, he thought. Yet, things had turned out darn well.

"Deepa," he said slipping another pillow behind his back, "you never asked me if I was with someone before you."

She didn't respond.

"Well...two American girls asked me out," he continued. "But I said NO."

She simply shook her head.

"What are you thinking?"

"Dipin, you are very honest."

"No, what are you really thinking?"

"Oh...so you would like to know if I...?"

"No pressure on you.... Really, I am not interested in your past."

"Dipin...."

"So, did you fall in love before?"

"What do you mean?"

"Before me, I mean...did you?"

"No."

"Did you?"

"Dipin...."

"Tell me it never happened."

"Dipin...."

"Is the answer NO?"

"Only once...Dipin."

Dipin felt molten worms crawling on him again. So she had a history after all. She was with a man. God, with some other man. It was like a movie he had watched recently.

"Do you have his photo?"

She didn't say a thing.

"Did you go the whole distance?"

"What do you mean?"

"All the way?"

She was quiet, almost petrified.

"And why...why didn't you marry this person?"

"I...," she said. "I...."

"You proposed?"

"Said...," she broke down. "The person wasn't attracted to me any more."

She watched him sneeze into a fistful of Kleenex. *Aa-chhe. Aa-chhe. Aa-chhe.*

"Dipin...I am sorry if this hurts you. That was a long time ago. That is why I left India for New York."

"And how long ago is long ago?"

"Dipin...it was long ago and now it doesn't matter...all over between that person and me."

"And why wasn't he interested in a beautiful woman like you?" he handed her a Kleenex.

"He told me...," she said, "She told me.... No, sorry.... He told me he was attracted only to men."

Deepa touched her ring finger and was silent until sleep sealed her on the sofa; her first sleep ever since she landed in America. On the table in front of her lay uneaten pasta in the silver tray. Her breath became lighter every time she exhaled because she was exhaling away the exhaustion of her long journey. He washed his face with cold water in the bathroom and then limped toward the window. The Titans stared back at him. He looked down 67 floors. Gaudy neon still flickered on the *Kiss Me Kelly* poster. He wondered how long the show would last. He heard a thunderous applause. It sounded like thousands of fire sirens. Angry, speeding, furious.

He felt like checking into a different room in the hotel. No, no, he said. Perhaps I ought to resume my relationship with this woman, he said. But how does one resume a thing that has barely begun? There were fireworks imploding his brain. He couldn't understand why he felt deceived and not deceived, both at once. Why did she have to tell him everything? Did she really tell him everything? Perhaps she was with a woman. No, no, it is just not practical—to be turned on by a woman. And yet what a relief it would be to know for certain that she was only with a woman. Most certainly she was with a man. How dare she be with a different man? How dare she have been with someone who wasn't even attracted to her? How was it possible? A man not attracted to a beautiful woman?

He slapped himself rapidly until the cheeks reddened. He rushed back to the bathroom. He saluted himself several times in front of the mirror. One thing I am not, he muttered. *I never was a narrowminded schmuck.* He splashed cold water on his face. Ten, fifteen, a hundred times. She should have kept it as a secret, he muttered.... Hurts me. Hurts her. Must have hurt him terribly, the other man. Oh the day the other man in her life must have gathered the courage to reveal that he was not attracted to her or to any other woman.... She must have been devastated...it, it must have provoked rashes on the other man's heart. Deepa must never tell her past to the CEO's wife. Never. The CEO of the chemical company must never find out about the other man.

Dipin heard a knock on the door.

The knock grew louder and louder.

—*Ma'am, Sir!*

"Respect the Don't Disturb sign," he yelled back.

—*The fire-alarm! Fire!*

They slithered through the Emergency spiral, clinging to the Filipino linen girls and the firemen. Stair after stair. Deepa's sari stuck in the railing but Dipin released it swiftly. They joined hundreds of panicked people who had been evacuated from the hotel rooms. Despite the September chill in the air his shirt smelled of sweat and turned black. His wife didn't have her sandals on. He had forgotten the cell phone and the keys in the room above. Flames scalded his eyelids, and left him completely dry.

"At least we are alive!" he muttered. "Alive and for each other."

The fleeing crowd forced them apart many times, but each time they found each other.

She vaguely recognized Dipin's ash-smeared face from distance. "That must be him." She glided past Broadway, barefooted, in that burgundy sari of hers and tapped on his shoulder.

"You must be my husband?" she asked.

"Of course," he said without a hint of hesitation.

She held his hand, and slowly quickened her step.

He followed—walking in the direction he did not know.

NEIL SMITH was born in Montreal and works there now as a translator. His stories have appeared widely in literary journals. He has been nominated for the Journey Prize twice as well as for this year's National Magazine Award for fiction.

MAUREEN BILERMAN lives in Fredericton. She is currently finishing her Masters degree in Creative Writing at the University of New Brunswick. Her story "Getaway" took first place in the New Brunswick Literary Competition in 2002.

JASPREET SINGH grew up in India and Kashmir. His stories have appeared in *Fiddlehead* and *Zoetrope*, and were nominated for publication in *Best New American Voices*. He lives in Montreal.

MARK ANTHONY JARMAN is the author of *Salvage King Ya!*, *New Orleans is Sinking*, *19 Knives* and *Ireland's Eye*. He has won the Gold Medal at the National Magazine Awards, and was a co-winner of the *Prism international* Short Fiction Contest. He is the fiction editor of *Fiddlehead* and teaches at UNB.

Previous volumes in this series contained stories by the following writers:

2003: Liam Durcan, Andrea Rudy, Jessica Grant
2002: Chris Labonté, Lawrence Mathews, Kelly Cooper
2001: J.A. McCormack, Ramona Dearing, Goran Simic
2000: Christine Erwin, Vivette J. Kady, Timothy Taylor
1999: Marcus Youssef, Mary Swan, John Lavery
1998: Leona Theis, Gabriella Goliger, Darryl Whetter
1997: Elyse Gasco, Dennis Bock, Nadine McInnis
1996: Lewis DeSoto, Murray Logan, Kelley Aitken
1995: Warren Cariou, Marilyn Gear Pilling, François Bonneville
1994: Donald McNeill, Elise Levine, Lisa Moore
1993: Gayla Reid, Hannah Grant, Barbara Parkin
1992: Caroline Adderson, Marilyn Eisenstat, Marina Endicott
1991: Ellen McKeough, Robert Majzels, Patricia Seaman
1990: Peter Stockland, Sara McDonald, Steven Heighton
1989: Brian Burke, Michelle Heinemann, Jean Rysstad
1988: Christopher Fisher, Carol Anne Wien, Rick Hillis
1987: Charles Foran, Patricia Bradbury, Cynthia Holz
1986: Dayv James-French, Lesley Krueger, Rohinton Mistry
1985: Sheila Delany, Frances Itani, Judith Pond
1984: Diane Schoemperlen, Joan Fern Shaw, Michael Rawdon
1983: Sharon Butala, Bonnie Burnard, Sharon Sparling
1982: Barry Dempster, Don Dickinson, Dave Margoshes
1981: Peter Behrens, Linda Svendsen, Ernest Hekkanen
1980: Martin Avery, Isabel Huggan, Mike Mason

Most of these books are still available. Please inquire.